Temptation of a Succubus

By Adrian Lopez

Trigger Warnings

THIS BOOK CONTAINS MULTIPLE EXAMPLES
OF, BUT NOT LIMITED TO.

MURDER
SEXUAL ASSAULT
RAPE
BLOOD PLAY
KNIFE PLAY
NECROPHILIA
DISMEMBERMENT
SEXUAL ASPHYXIATION
EATING BODY PARTS
EXPLICIT SEX SCENES
AMPUTATION
DEATH
SELF-HARM
SEXUAL ABUSE
TORTURE
KIDNAPPING
STALKING
VIOLENCE
GRAPHIC HORROR
GRAPHIC BODY HORROR
SWEARING

DEDICATION

This book is dedicated to all the readers out there. Those that came for the romance but stayed for the dark. Those who were intrigued with the horror but craved the erotic. Those who just wanted to curl up with their favorite blanket and beverage to read. That just wanted the simple: tentacle sex, tall tattooed kidnapper, stalker, being choked, tied up, serial killer, knife play, paranormal demon romance storylines. Bathed in layers upon layers of spice. With an unapologetic love for those dark, twisted, and spicy words. This is for you!

"Camilla, with her eyes like twilight's embrace, dances between the realms of sweetest dreams and most haunting nightmares—where her love can envelop you in a tender kiss or leave you shivering in the shadow of desire's darkest depths."

"With deliberate precision,
he traced deep cuts along his inner thigh,
each slice a symphony of agony and ecstasy
that elicited soft moans from him."

CHAPTER 1

Lucia

He grabbed the knife from his nightstand, the cold steel a familiar comfort against his skin. With deliberate precision, he traced deep cuts along his inner thigh, each slice a symphony of agony and ecstasy that elicited soft moans from him. Intoxicated by the raw pleasure coursing through his veins, he brought the blade to his lips, savoring the taste of his own blood as it danced on his tongue.

The moment the metallic tang hit his senses, arousal surged through him, leaving him fully erect. Placing the blade gently beside him on the bed, he coated his hand with the warm crimson liquid seeping from his wounds. He began to stroke himself, using his blood as lubricant.

Lost in the hypnotic rhythm of his movements, Emiliano closed his eyes, only to feel an icy touch around his cock and a warm breath against the nape of his neck.

"Let me help you with that, Emiliano, my love," came Camilla's sultry voice—a melody of darkness and desire.

Her cold hand slithered across his shoulders before settling firmly over his throat. Her fingers elongated unnaturally, tightening their grip until each breath became a struggle for survival. Sharp nails glided down his torso with merciless precision, leaving thin rivulets of blood in their wake.

A cold grasp wrenched Emiliano's wrist away from himself. He watched in mesmerized desire as the blood coating his erection morphed into Camilla's hand. She began stroking him with torturous expertise that married pain and pleasure in perfect harmony.

Her serpentine tongue flickered into his ear, whispering seductively, "Yesss! Think about her, my love... her cries for mercy... her dying breath." Her final words dissolved into a serpentine hiss that sent shivers down Emiliano's spine and straight into his cock.

Obediently, Emiliano let Camilla's words guide him back into memories of their recent violence. He recalled walking along the Spanish hillside when he had spotted her, an unsuspecting beauty named Lucia traveling alone.

The thrill of anticipation had been intoxicating as he tracked her every step from a distance. It wasn't enough to simply kill; he craved the fear that flickered in their eyes at the moment they realized their fate was sealed by him.

As they neared a secluded wooded area, he closed in like a predator, ready to pounce on its prey. Lucia had been distracted when she collided with him, falling gracelessly at his feet.

She looked up slowly to find herself before a striking figure over six feet tall; tattoos adorned much of his muscular frame but spared his chiseled face a mask of dangerous allure. S-Sorry... I didn't see you there," she stammered nervously while gathering herself off the ground.

Emiliano offered her an outstretched hand accompanied by an inviting smile—a stark contrast to what lay beneath it all. "You shouldn't be out here after dark," he advised smoothly while helping brush dirt off of her clothes, his touch lingering longer than necessary—"I'm actually heading home too; let me walk you."

In her naive trustfulness, or perhaps blinded by charm alone—Lucia accepted graciously: Thank you. I'm Lucia by name."

It's lovely meeting you, Lucía," replied Emiliano warmly before placing reverent kisses upon the backhand, setting the stage perfectly for what cruel game was yet to unfold thereafter...

They walked along the road under a canopy of stars, their conversation light but laden with unspoken tension. After twenty minutes, they reached a densely wooded area where Emiliano abruptly halted.

"What's wrong? Do you hear something?" Lucia asked nervously.

"Yes, Lucia," Emiliano replied, his voice tinged with a sinister undercurrent. Something inevitable is coming. I can hear it clearly—it echoes in my ears. He closed his eyes, a predatory smirk curling his lips.

"But I don't hear anything," Lucia protested.

"That's because what I'm hearing hasn't happened yet," he murmured, opening his eyes that now gleamed with dark intent. "What I hear are your cries for help, your pointless, hysterical cries for help!"

Before she could react, Emiliano shoved her down an embankment. Her scream pierced the night air as she landed roughly at the bottom.

"Ahhh, there they are! A beautiful symphony to my ears, he said as he descended towards her with deliberate slowness.

His demeanor had transformed; gone was the charming man she had been speaking with. His eyes were now black voids, filled with malevolent intent. Lucia blinked rapidly; was she hallucinating? Over his shoulder loomed a beautiful woman shrouded in mist, whispering into his ear. For a fleeting moment, fear gave way to an inexplicable desire to see more of this ethereal figure.

Emiliano grabbed Lucia by her throat and ripped off her long coat before throwing her back onto it on the ground. He leaned close enough for her to smell his breath, ripe with sadistic excitement.

I'm going to enjoy this far more than you will, my beautiful Lucia," he hissed as he tore at her clothes with a feral intensity.

A cold whisper reached his ear: Let me help you, my love. Camilla appeared from a swirling black mist and kneeled over Lucia. Before she could scream again, Camilla shoved her thick black tail down Lucia's throat, silencing her cries and filling her mouth completely.

Lucia's body convulsed as Camilla moaned in ecstasy, holding her hands apart so Emiliano could proceed unhindered.

With surgical precision, he carved circles around each of Lucia's breasts before connecting them with a line down to her navel. He retrieved a plastic bag from his pocket and meticulously sliced off each nipple, placing them inside with care fit for an artist.

Despite her writhing pain, Camilla's tail kept moving in and out of Lucia's throat while Camilla's moans grew louder.

Emiliano sealed the bag and marked it with "Lucia," followed by a black heart drawing before pocketing it once again. He then freed himself from his pants, arousal evident from the torment inflicted upon their captive.

Blood poured from fresh cuts on Lucia's legs as Emiliano reveled in their shared cruelty. Camilla's forked tongue slid into Emiliano's mouth as they kissed fervently, their passion intensifying alongside the throbbing cock between his legs.

Emiliano's fingers traced Camilla's dark wings as they lay entwined on bloodstained sheets. "Do you remember our last dance with Lucia?" His whisper was soft yet charged with dark intent.

Camilla's eyes gleamed with recollection and lust as she gazed at him through half-lidded eyes. "How could I forget? Her screams were our symphony."

The room was thick with the scent of iron and sweat—a testament to their recent indulgence. As Emiliano closed his eyes and remembered as he moved closer to where Lucia's lifeless body still lay, he felt a rush of exhilaration mixed with arousal.

He kneeled beside her, running his hands over her cooling skin before parting her legs once more. "One last time," he murmured, positioning himself at her entrance.

Meanwhile, Camilla's tail slithered across Lucia's corpse, moving deliberately until it reached her throat again. Each thrust made Lucia's jaw slacken further in deathly compliance.

"Patience," Camilla purred at Emiliano's eager movements below them both. "We have all night."

As Emiliano plunged into Lucia's yielding body once more, goosebumps erupted across his skin at how perfectly tight she remained even in death, his own perverse form of worshiping what they had created together.

His mind raced; every thrust brought him closer, not only physically but emotionally bound deeper in this twisted love affair they reveled in so much.

Camilla mounted Emiliano, bringing him back from the memory of Lucia—her eyes glowing red-hot while demon-like talons dug fiercely into Emiliano's calves, pulling them apart effortlessly. Showing off raw, unearthly strength that only heightened Emiliano's agonizing pleasures, further subjugating willingly under such forbidden dominance displayed flawlessly before him. Entirely now caught entrancingly within beautifully demonic form, completely taking control thrillingly atop him. Emiliano gasped intensely, grasping just barely enough air to continue breathing. While still feeling Camilla's pussy tighten rhythmically and hungrily consuming his pulsating erect cock as she continued riding fervently...

"The young man was exquisite—
the things I did to him."
She moaned softly, tracing her fingers down
Emiliano's arm provocatively."

CHAPTER 2

Married Couple

The town slowly gathered in the wooded area outside of town. Whispers of a young girl's mutilated body found by the roadside had circulated all morning like a morbid wind. Spain's National Police roped off the area, shielding the victim's remains from prying eyes while officers huddled together discussing grim details.

The officer in charge scanned the crowd, his gaze landing on a striking couple who stood out starkly amidst familiar faces. The man towered at six foot five with hair elegantly combed back, his muscular frame barely concealed by an expensive suit. His companion was equally arresting; her skin-tight red dress accentuated voluptuous curves under a cascade of jet-black hair.

Their eyes glittered with an unsettling excitement as they surveyed the scene before them.

"Get a statement from those two," the head officer commanded brusquely.

"Who, sir? There's nobody there," one officer replied.

Startled, he looked over again—only to find them gone. They had vanished without a trace, feeding into his growing suspicion that these enigmatic strangers were involved in ways yet unknown.

Intent on unraveling this mystery, the police captain stormed into town straight to its main tourist hotel.

"They checked in five days ago," said the young desk clerk dreamily after hearing their description. Paid in cash for an entire month... She was unforgettable."

The captain took the key and room number with grim resolve, summoning backup before heading to the secluded bungalow at the edge of the property.

Inside lay a chilling spectacle: a naked young man bound face-down on the bed with long, deep claw marks etched across his back like grotesque trophies. His throat bore bruises from something large that had strangled him; his legs were spread wide open, exposing raw tears around his anal area from a brutal penetration that left behind blood and an ominous black fluid seeping from within him.

"Captain, you have to see this over here!" one of the officers called from the bathroom. As the captain entered, his gaze locked onto a young woman strung up by her hands to the showerhead. Her throat was slit, blood trailing down her body in macabre rivulets, mingling with the numerous slashes carved into her flesh. Her nipples had been surgically removed; evidence matched what they found on the body in the woods. Signs of sexual assault were evident, marked by blood and fluids; however, not with the sheer brutality inflicted on the young man on the bed.

A knot tightened in the captain's stomach—he knew he was closing in on them. The couple from the woods were undoubtedly behind these monstrous acts. Gathering evidence meticulously, he recalled what he'd learned from the front desk clerk—a newlywed couple had checked in that same day. They had been seen socializing with the suspects several nights ago. Their room was ransacked; all valuables and their rental car were missing. He immediately issued an alert to search for that car in neighboring towns.

"The view is so beautiful from here, mi amor," Emiliano murmured to Camilla as they stood at the cliff's edge, bathed in the dying light of sunset.

Camilla's eyes sparkled wickedly as she replied, "I'll miss that town—it was delicious fun." She licked her lips sensually. That sweet little bag of flesh in the woods... my tail longs for that tight little throat of hers." She giggled, a sound both alluring and chilling. "And that married couple... Ah! The young man was exquisite—the things I did to him." She moaned softly, tracing her fingers down Emiliano's arm provocatively.

Emiliano's gaze darkened with lustful remembrance as he fingered a small baggie from his pocket. "Ah yes, my beautiful little Cintia," he whispered, gazing lovingly at the severed nipples within.

Camilla sauntered behind their stolen car effortlessly, pushing it over the cliff's edge, while Emiliano watched with an admiring smile. The vehicle vanished into the dense forest below; it would be years before anyone discovered it amidst those shadows.

"On to our next adventure, my love," Camilla laughed melodiously, wrapping herself around Emiliano—her arm around his neck while her sinuous tail coiled possessively around his waist.

Embracing each other intimately, they walked into the encroaching darkness—hungry for their next indulgence in perverse pleasure.

"Stop whining, you know you love Mama's demon dick! Now take it like a good boy!" she commanded. His pleas were cut off as Camilla's tail shot through his mouth, ending his life instantly."

CHAPTER 3

Las Tres Lindas

It had been months since they discreetly left Spain, quietly making their way through Europe, indulging in the sights and savoring the local "delicacies." For them, though, those delicacies rarely came from a menu.

Now, they found themselves seated in a charming café in Capri, overlooking the serene ocean. Camilla's eyes had already settled on her next craving. Across the café, three young, beautiful Italian women sat in a corner, casting glances at Emiliano and giggling amongst themselves. Camilla, noticing their interest, waved a waiter over.

"Yes, ma'am?" the waiter asked as he approached.

"I'd like you to send your most expensive bottle of champagne to that table over there, with las tres lindas," Camilla instructed, nodding subtly toward the women.

"Absolutely, ma'am. But, if I may ask, what does 'las tres lindas' mean?" The waiter inquired, a bit perplexed.

Camilla flashed him a dazzling smile. "Oh, I'm sorry, darling. I forgot I'm in Italy, not Spain. It means 'the three beautiful ladies.'"

The waiter, momentarily entranced by her beauty, hesitated before finally tearing his gaze away to fulfill her request.

"What are you plotting now, mi amor?" Emiliano asked, a hint of amusement in his voice.

"We just had lunch, my love. I'm arranging for dessert," Camilla replied with a sly grin. "When the waiter delivers the champagne, raise your glass to them when they turn around."

Moments later, the waiter approached the women's table with the champagne, informing them of the generous gesture. The women turned to look, their faces lighting up with wide smiles as they giggled together.

They had been practically eye fucking Emiliano from the moment they sat down. He gave them a devilish grin, raising his glass in a silent toast before beckoning them over. Without hesitation, they gathered their things and made their way to the table, whispering excitedly as they approached. Emiliano rose to greet them, offering a gentle kiss on each of their hands. "My name is Emiliano, and this stunning woman beside me is Camilla. And what might your names be, beautiful ladies?" he asked, his voice smooth and inviting.

"I'm Alessandra, and these are my friends, Gabriella and Alessia," the most confident of the three responded.

"Why don't you sit here next to me, Alessandra? And you two can join Emiliano," Camilla suggested, her eyes already set on her desired dessert.

As Alessandra sat down, Camilla's hand slid softly down her back, resting on her butt. With a slow, deliberate motion, she brushed Alessandra's hair aside, leaning in to kiss her deeply. Alessandra's knees buckled slightly, the intensity of the moment overwhelming her.   It was impossible to resist Camilla's advances.

Meanwhile, Emiliano held out chairs for Gabriella and Alessia, seating them on either side of him. They exchanged knowing smiles, sensing that the evening was about to take an interesting turn. Camilla waved the waiter over to their table.

"I'd like to buy out the remaining tables on the terrace for the next hour or so. I don't want to be disturbed. There will be a generous tip when we're done," she instructed.

"Of course, ma'am," the waiter replied quickly, rushing off to fulfill her request. Emiliano and his companions turned their attention to the spectacle unfolding before them as Camilla and Alessandra passionately made out at the table.

Camilla deftly slipped the straps of Alessandra's dress off her shoulders, revealing her beautiful natural breasts. She licked her nipples softly, rolling her tongue around them before pausing to suck gently. Alessandra could only tilt her head back and moan, completely lost in the sensations

Camilla was evoking. As Camilla continued to lavish attention on her breasts, her hands wandered down to Alessandra's inner thighs. Every touch sent waves of pleasure through Alessandra, making her wetter by the second, uncaring that they were in a public space.

Meanwhile, Emiliano was fully engaged with Gabriella and Alessia. Gabriella had already freed his erect cock. and was stroking it under the table. Alessia joined in, their petite hands working in tandem. Emiliano's hands wandered up their dresses, swiftly yanking off their panties. Both girls squealed with delight at his forceful touch. Their inner thighs were already soaked, making it easy for Emiliano to slide his fingers inside their tight, wet pussies. They let out low, deep moans as he pushed his fingers in as far as they would go, his cock growing harder with each squeeze of their tight grips.

As their bodies shook with the intensity of their orgasms, Emiliano began to massage their clits with his thumbs. They tried to squirm away, overwhelmed by the strongest orgasms they had ever experienced, but

Emiliano held them in place, drawing out their pleasure.

At this moment, Alessandra was lost in her own private realm of ecstasy with Camilla. She was so immersed in the passion of the moment that she barely noticed when Camilla's tail began to penetrate her wanting pussy. Gripping the chair tightly, Alessandra surrendered to the rhythm of Camilla's tail as it thickened and pressed deeper with each thrust. The sensation of being so thoroughly filled was unlike anything she had ever felt; the stretch and depth were nearly overwhelming. She was unable to stop her relentless climaxing, each surge of pleasure leaving her further untethered and adrift. Camilla showered Alessandra's exquisite breasts with attention, her lips and hands incessantly caressing and teasing as she tilted Alessandra's head back in utter submission. Alessandra's body became a conduit for Camilla's desires, wholly surrendering to her every touch.

Meanwhile, Emiliano's attention was divided between Gabriella and Alessia. Both girls had moved to their knees before him, taking turns pleasuring him while the other attended to his balls. Camilla's wings began to form and extended towards the girls. Normally spiked, the tips of her wings transformed into large, hard cocks, rivaling Emiliano's. She entered both girls from behind, thrusting with her wings as she leaned back in her chair, moaning deeply. The sensation of Camilla's tail continued to drive Alessandra to multiple climaxes, while Gabriella and Alessia screamed in delight from the relentless thrusts of the wings.

With one hand, Camilla explored her own demon pussy, fingering herself and playing with her large clit as she continued to dominate all three women. As Emiliano neared his climax, he held Alessia's head firmly, burying his cock deep in her throat as he came repeatedly. Only pulling out when he was finished, he left Alessia gasping and choking. Gabriella quickly moved to clean Emiliano's cock, ensuring not a single drop was wasted.

Seeing Emiliano's dominance and knowing the state of Alessandra, Camilla was pushed to her own climax. She gushed dark black fluid as she fingered herself, and her tail pumped the same fluid deeply. into Alessandra. At that moment, Camilla noticed the waiter had been watching. Frightened, the waiter tried to flee, but Camilla reappeared in front of him, now in her human form.

"Where do you think you're going?" she asked, her voice dripping with menace.

"I—I didn't see anything, I promise! Just let me go, I won't say a word!" the waiter pleaded.

"Oh, I know you saw everything and enjoyed it," Camilla said, eyeing the wet spot on his pants. "You wish you were part of it, don't you?" She pushed him to the floor, licking the wet spot. "Don't worry, I'll take care of you," she said with a laugh as her wings flipped him onto his stomach. With her clawed hands, she ripped his pants off, exposing him.

As a stream of urine trickled down his leg, Camilla's playtime was just beginning. "Be a good boy for Mama!" she laughed, dragging her talons down his back.

"No, please!" he screamed.

"Now, now. I thought you'd be good for Mama! I won't tell you again—no noise. It distracts me!" She growled in a guttural voice. Extending her long black tongue, she licked his balls from behind and wrapped it around his cock, stroking it with her demon tongue.

"No, please!" he begged again.

"Mama told you, didn't she?" She snarled as her tail began to stretch out. She spread his ass cheeks and pushed her tail deep inside him. As she fucked him harder and faster, the tail became fully engorged. "Stop whining; you know you love Mama's demon dick! Now take it like a good boy!" she commanded. His pleas were cut off as Camilla's tail shot through his mouth, ending his life instantly.

"That's how Mama likes it—nice and quiet while she works," she moaned. Ramming her thick tail through his lifeless body. As she neared her own climax, she held his mouth closed, filling his entire body with her dark cum. When finished, she withdrew her tail, letting his body drop to the floor, black fluid flowing from both ends.

Returning to the table, she saw the three girls, now bent over the table with their nipples removed, their names—Alessandra, Gabriella, and Alessia—written on a plastic bag. Emiliano was still engaged with Alessandra's lifeless body, and Camilla, frustrated, bent down to help. She began to pleasure Emiliano's ass with her tongue, prompting him to finish inside Alessandra.

"Now get dressed. We need to leave this beautiful city quickly!" Camilla said as she grabbed Emiliano's arm, and they hurried away.

"Daddy can't hear you. He growled low
in her ear while tightening his hold on her waist.
"Do you want Daddy's dick or not?"

CHAPTER 4

Amalia

They grabbed all their belongings and headed down the elevator. It opened up to an absolutely stunning lobby filled with natural plants and several lounge areas where conversations flowed freely among tourists swarming Capri this season.

"Why don't you go see if you can find us some transportation, mi amor? I will check us out of the hotel and plan our next destination," Emiliano said, pressing a lingering kiss on Camilla's hand.

"Yes, my love," Camilla responded with a sultry smile as she sauntered through the lobby. Eyes followed her every step; her beauty was magnetic, almost otherworldly. Her presence was like witnessing an enchanting yet terrible spectacle; people were drawn in despite themselves.

Camilla exited through the front door, and only then did life resume its normal pace inside the lobby. Emiliano observed it all with a grin—she was his intoxicating enigma wrapped in pure sin.

After checking out, Emiliano turned to leave but was momentarily halted by the sight of a young woman standing to the side, her smile inviting. Though he was in a hurry, he felt an intense attraction building. His pants tightened noticeably, a fact made clear by her eyes wandering and the subtle lick of her lips. He asked the desk to hold their belongings, turning to face his prey. Then, with a deliberate, predatory elegance, he approached the young woman.

The woman appeared nervous, her usual confidence shaken by Emiliano's directness. Standing before her, Emiliano smirked, his lips parted in a grin. "Hi," she said, her voice tinged with apprehension. Emiliano wrapped an arm around her waist, pulling her close, and kissed her deeply, his touch both commanding and passionate.

"There's an out-of-service restroom over there. We're going to walk hand in hand to it. Once we're inside, I'm going to fuck you. I'm going to show you pleasures you never knew you needed. I'll take you in every way," he said in a deep, authoritative tone. She nodded, clearly eager.

Her breath hitched at his words; she nodded meekly.

Daddy can't hear you. He growled low in her ear while tightening his hold on her waist. "Do you want Daddy's dick or not?"

"Yes, daddy! I want you to fuck me with your fat cock!" She moaned breathlessly.

He led her towards the restroom, his arm firmly around her. After ensuring no one was watching, they entered. As soon as the door was closed, Emiliano lifted her into his arms and kissed her fervently. Guiding her over to the largest stall. He pushed her gently to her knees, instructing her to demonstrate her affection for him.

"Show me how much you love Daddy's cock," he commanded huskily.

She fumbled eagerly with his belt before freeing him from its confines, a primal hunger igniting within those previously timid eyes as she took his cock into mouth inch by inch until tears streamed down her cheeks from gagging. Emiliano's hands gripped her head, thrusting deeper, his moans mixing with her gagging. "That's my good girl," he encouraged, as he continued to guide her through the act.

Afterward, he spun her around and lowered her pants, bending to pleasure her. Her moans intensified as he explored her with his tongue and hands, leaving a red mark with a firm spank. "Tell me what you want," he commanded, his voice raw with desire.

"I want you to fuck me!" she screamed in response. Emiliano obliged, entering her with force, the intensity of their encounter echoing within the restroom. His grip on her arms and hips tightened as he drove deeper, each thrust eliciting more pleasure and pain.

As she climaxed, Emiliano did not relent, continuing his relentless pace until she could no longer maintain her grip. He withdrew, allowing her a moment to recover before moving on to a new level of intimacy. Gently, he began to choke her while fucking her from behind. Her cries were a mix of pleasure and distress as he pushed his full length inside her.

Eventually, he withdrew, her body slumping to the ground. Emiliano retrieved her purse, noting her name, "Amalia," and collected a trophy—a bag containing her nipples. He pocketed it and left the restroom, heading to collect his belongings.

"Over in Spain, there is a hacienda looking for a caretaker," said the stranger into his phone. "It's secluded—La Hacienda Aparicio. Nobody visits year-round. I'll be heading there tonight. You won't hear from me for a while." He ended the call and began walking out of the dimly lit hotel lobby.

Emiliano trailed after him silently until they reached an alley shrouded in shadows. With calculated ease he approached. "Excuse me, sorry to bother you," Emiliano said smoothly. The stranger turned, polite curiosity in his eyes as he looked at Emiliano's phone screen displaying a map.

"I was trying to find my way to Palermo," Emiliano continued, stepping closer. As soon as the man leaned in, Emiliano struck his blade effortlessly, slicing into flesh multiple times before any cry could escape. The stranger crumpled silently; no one would hear his final breath amidst the city's noise.

Emiliano dragged him behind some barrels before wiping his blade clean on his coat, whistling softly as he rounded the corner back towards his beloved Camilla, waiting by a sleek car.

Camilla stood by an open door, breathtaking even in her monstrous form—a vision of beauty marred by darkness as she expertly peeled strips of skin from her prey in rhythmic motions. Her tail writhed sensuously; dark fluid pumped into her victim, who lay half-dead yet unable to scream—an offering rendered silent under her spell.

"Oh, my love! You startled me," she purred upon seeing him approach, her form seamlessly shifting back into its alluring human guise. "This generous young man offered us his vehicle," she added with laughter that echoed like silk over steel.

Emiliano couldn't help but chuckle at her playful demeanor despite the gruesome scene. "Mi amor, he teased gently after placing their bags inside. You really must learn to be cleaner. He wiped off smeared blood mixed with her black cum from the seats with practiced ease before settling beside her.

"Never mind that now," he murmured against her ear as the engine roared beneath them. A beast eager for freedom much like themselves—our new destination awaits amongst the beautiful Spanish countryside. With one last glance at the discarded remains left behind (a stark reminder of their power), they drove off into night wrapped tightly around secrets meant only for lovers entwined by darkness' embrace...

"That's Daddy's little demon slut!"
Emiliano growled, his voice low and dripping with
possessive hunger. He leaned forward,
his tongue flicking out to tease her tail as it
plunged deeper inside her."

CHAPTER 5

The Hitchhikers

Emiliano cruised along the countryside road, windows down, music drifting in the breeze. He couldn't help but admire Camilla, her long, straight black hair dancing in the wind like dark ocean waves. She turned and smiled knowingly at him; her allure was undeniable.

"Dammit, my love! You promised you wouldn't use your demon's glamor on me!" Emiliano protested, a mix of annoyance and admiration in his voice.

"Don't be mad, Daddy," Camilla cooed, leaning close, her demon tongue playfully tracing his ear and neck, her kisses soft yet charged with intent. "Let me make it up to you, please," she whispered seductively, her voice barely concealing the menace beneath.

Emiliano's breath caught in his throat, his grip on the steering wheel tightening for a moment before he surrendered to the pull of her touch and the world outside the car vanishing as he sank back into the seat, drawn to her like a moth to flame." As Camilla's hands daringly ventured into his pants, pulling out his erect cock.

Gently stroking it, she licked her lips. "I'm yours, Daddy, but this belongs to me," she murmured, her eyes locked on his, as her tongue, unnaturally long and serpentine, coiled around his cock with a slow, deliberate possessiveness that sent a shiver of both arousal and unease through him. She tenderly kissed it and softly drew him in, her lips and tongue working in a harmonious rhythm.

Emiliano was aware that his size often startled most, with its impressive length and girth. Most lovers faltered, their eyes widening as they tried and failed to take him fully, but Camilla's eyes only gleamed with hunger. She devoured him with a confidence that bordered on otherworldly. Her lips never hesitating, her breath steady as if she were savoring every inch of him. Her tongue continued to stroke his cock as she took him into her mouth. Emiliano shivered as the tip of his dick touched the back of her throat; then, seamlessly, she deepened the embrace, taking him deeper inside her. A moan escaped him, "Fuck, my love," as he felt her lips graze his balls. Her throat seemed to clasp around him, massaging along the entire length of his cock as she drew him deeper inside her.

As the journey continued, Emiliano's focus wavered under the spell of Camilla's relentless affection. He had to pull over, overwhelmed by sensations he'd never before experienced. Her throat was literally milking his cock, drawing him deeper with every motion, and he was lost in the wild intensity of the sensation, trying not to cum.

Just as his body teetered on the edge of release, Camilla's tongue coiled around his balls with knowing restraint, holding him back, savoring the power she had over him in that exact moment, her eyes gleaming with the delight of drawing out his torment. Yet, caught in the heat of the moment, Emiliano knew nothing could hold back the impending release.

He grasped her silky black hair, holding her head down tightly as he clenched his ass cheeks, releasing everything he had down her throat. But even after the last drop,

Camilla didn't stop. She craved more, moving deeper and faster on his cock. The sensation was unlike anything he had ever experienced, and he climaxed again and again. Finally, Camilla surfaced, giving him a deep, lingering kiss, her demon tongue still coated with his cum.

"You owe me big time, Daddy!" Camilla purred, her voice dripping with playful menace as she sank into the seat. A subtle rustle of fabric hinted at the emergence of her tail, its tip curling suggestively before tracing the curve of her thigh, slowly sliding down to caress her waiting pussy. A low moan escaped her lips, breathy and soft, as her fingers danced over the supple swell of her breasts.

"Feed me, Daddy," she whispered, her voice thick with hunger. Her body quivered with every breath, each inhale deepening the flush on her cheeks as heat pooled low in her belly.

They began to drive down the road to find a place to pull over and not be disturbed. Emiliano noticed two Spanish girls hitchhiking along the side. "I've got a little treat for you, my love," Emiliano murmured, his voice a low rumble as his eyes glinted with mischief. "But you might want to soften those edges—don't want to scare off the goodies," he said with a playful wink.

A ripple of shadow passed over Camilla's features, her true form momentarily flickering like a predator hidden in plain sight, before she settled back into her flawless human guise. The shift was so seamless it was as if the darkness had only been a trick of the light. Emiliano pulled over, and Camilla rolled down the window. "Are you lovely ladies looking for a ride?" she asked, flashing them a seductive smile. Unbeknownst to them, they were already ensnared in her glamor. Smiling back, they took her hand and climbed into the back seat.

Emiliano's gaze flickered to the rearview mirror, where he caught sight of Camilla's delicate fingers weaving through their hair, guiding them to her breasts. The soft, wet sounds of lips meeting skin filled the car, blending with the hum of the engine. She met his eyes in the mirror, a mischievous smile playing on her lips. "Drive, my love.

And take your time," she murmured, her voice a sultry command that sent a shiver down his spine.

Emiliano's grip tightened on the steering wheel, his knuckles whitening as he struggled to keep his focus on the road. The three women in the back were stunning—silken skin glistening in the low light, curves that seemed to defy gravity. A surge of lust tugged at his restraint, threatening to pull him under. His focus wavered as he watched Camilla's fingers, darkened by the shadow of her true form, curled around their nipples, squeezing with a pressure that bordered on cruel. The women gasped, but their eyes remained glazed, trapped in the rapture of her glamor. In that blissful haze, they couldn't feel the sharp edge of her touch—the wicked joy that flickered in Camilla's eyes as she tightened her grip.

She laid them down on their backs, her eyes gleaming with wicked intent as she moved lower. Slowly, she dragged her talons from their breasts down to their stomachs, leaving deep, deliberate marks in her wake. Camilla's forked tongue trailed over the young woman's quivering skin, each slow stroke a calculated dance between pleasure and pain, her eyes glittering with the dark promise of what she could do.

Slowly, Camilla's tongue descended further down the young woman's trembling body, tasting the soft salt of her skin. She lingered at the edge of her folds, each breath drawing a shiver from the woman beneath her—an unspoken plea for more. As she circled the throbbing bud, the air between them thickened, electric with unsaid promises. Camilla didn't rush; she savored the journey, every inch a dance of slick heat and pulsing want. The woman's thighs quivered, parting wider, welcoming the invasion with a desperate ache that only Camilla could soothe.

The deeper it went, the more she explored every inch, focusing on the sweet spot that made the woman quiver with pleasure. With a slow withdrawal, Camilla turned her attention to the other girl, letting her tongue work its magic until both were soaked from the sinful caress.

Camilla's fingers began to twirl, the nails retracting as her index and middle fingers merged, thickening and forming a curved, rounded head. She eased them into the girls, slowly at first, but soon quickened the pace, thrusting deeper and harder. The twisting, pulsing mass of her fingers drove them wild, their bodies convulsing as waves of ecstasy crashed over them, one orgasm after another.

A deep, guttural moan escaped Camilla, almost feral in its intensity. The sight of her pleasure was too much for Emiliano; he unzipped his pants, releasing his throbbing cock. Over his shoulder, he caught a glimpse of Camilla's tongue, now slithering down his chest, coiling around his shaft to taste the pre-cum that had gathered from watching the erotic scene unfold. Camilla's moan reverberated through her chest, low and primal, as the salty tang of Emiliano's pre-cum coated her tongue. It wasn't just pleasure—it was the intoxicating flavor of power she craved.

Unable to resist, Emiliano pulled the car over, parking behind a screen of trees. Leaning back, he surrendered to Camilla's tongue as it stroked his aching cock. "Fuck me, my love. Give me what is mine!" Camilla growled, her voice thick with desire.

Emiliano didn't need to be told twice. He climbed out of the car and opened the back door, his eyes locking onto Camilla's inviting curves—her ass and pussy were beckoning him. Bending down, he thrust his tongue into her ass, devouring her with feral intensity. She moaned deeply, every movement sparking sensations she had never felt before with any other mortal. There was something about Emiliano's dark, twisted soul that ignited her craving.

As he feasted on Camilla's pussy, she was lost in a haze of pleasure, ramming her fingers faster and faster into the girls, their moans filling the air. Kneeling behind her, Emiliano dipped his hand into the folds of her wet pussy, coating it with her black juices that were dripping out. Stroking his cock, getting it nice and wet for her, he prepared to enter her. He stroked his cock, preparing for her, before delivering a teasing slap to her ass.

"Please, daddy, fuck me!" she moaned, and he obliged, sliding himself deep inside her. Gripping her hips, he thrust hard and fast, giving her exactly what she craved. The sight of the girls, lost in their unending waves of ecstasy, only fueled his desire, making his cock swell with each thrust. Emiliano brought his hand down on Camilla's ass, the sharp crack of his hand against her flesh echoed in the air. The sting blossomed into a delicious burn that made her gasp. Pain danced with pleasure, intertwining until she couldn't tell where one ended and the other began.

"I want you to fuck your own ass for Daddy," Emiliano commanded, his voice dark and commanding.

Camilla moaned at the thought, her tail emerging and lengthening. When it was thick and strong enough, Emiliano grabbed it, spit on it, and guided it into her ass. As he spread her cheeks and drove himself deeper into her, he growled, "Fuck your ass for Daddy!"

Without hesitation, Camilla began ramming her own tail deep into herself, matching his pace.

"Deeper, baby, and much, much thicker!" Emiliano commanded, his voice ragged with lust.

Her tail thickened further, stretching her even more as it coiled deeper inside her. The sensation was overwhelming—a sinuous serpent that filled her with every pulse, twisting and turning, each movement reinforcing both the power she wielded and the submission she craved.

"That's Daddy's little demon slut!" Emiliano growled, his voice low and dripping with possessive hunger. He leaned forward, his tongue flicking out to tease her tail as it plunged deeper inside her.

Camilla's wings flared open, muscles tensing, pressing against the leather seat as if her very skin couldn't contain the heat coursing through her. Her spine bowed, back arching in a desperate attempt to embrace the searing ecstasy that burned through her every nerve. She was being ravaged, fucked like never before—by both Emiliano and herself—each thrust pushing her closer to the edge. The low growl that escaped her lips grew louder, primal, as she felt the climax building within her.

Emiliano's breath hitched, a guttural sound escaping his throat as her tail coiled around his cock, its touch electrifying. Each subtle stroke against him sent waves of sharp, unrelenting need coursing through his veins, threatening to unravel him entirely.

Her tight, wet pussy clenched around him with a possessive force, every pulse pulling him further into the abyss. His body coiled tight, the pressure building until, with a ragged cry, the tension snapped, flooding her with everything he had, his dark essence pouring out in a torrent.

His seed, thick and malevolent, seeped into her, a cold fire igniting deep within as her hunger flared, greedy for every last drop. Her body quivered, alive with the dark energy that only he could give her—a sustenance that made her feel whole, powerful, and unstoppable. But one load was never enough for Camilla. Her greedy cunt continued to work his cock, milking him for more as she came, her own juices flooding her ass and leaking around her tail.

Emiliano watched, captivated, as the thick black cum oozed from her ass, the sight both terrifying and intoxicating. Weak from the relentless pleasure, he could do nothing but surrender to her. His fingers dipped into the slick mess, scooping up her essence, and brought it to his lips. The moment her demonic cum touched his tongue, his mind exploded with visions—orgies of demons and humans, pleasure so intense it consumed him entirely.

When Camilla's pussy finally released its vice-like grip, Emiliano snapped back to reality. Shakily, he stepped out of the car, leaning forward to lick her ass, savoring the taste of her one last time. "They're all yours, mi amor. My gift to you," he whispered, pressing a reverent kiss to her perfect ass before closing the car door.

Exhausted, Emiliano found a soft patch of grass beneath a tree and collapsed. He needed to recover after that wild session.

From inside the car, Camilla's feral growls echoed as she moved, the sound sending a thrill down his spine. The air inside the car grew thick, almost stifling, as the windows fogged with a sinister red mist. Emiliano's lips curled into a satisfied smirk, his pulse quickening at the wet, tearing sounds that followed—a symphony of flesh and bone being devoured. Camilla's feral growls reverberated through the car, and the knowledge that she was feeding, indulging in her dark hunger, sent a thrill through him that he couldn't—and wouldn't—deny.

A succubus needed semen to survive. Folktales painted them as creatures who visited men in their sleep, draining them with sex until they were spent. Camilla had explained it all to him when they first met. A succubus formed a bond with the man she fed from repeatedly, and after the countless victims they had shared, their bond was nearly unbreakable. Men came and went, their bodies mere vessels for fleeting pleasure, their essence nothing more than a bitter aftertaste to her. But with Emiliano, it was different—his touch set her aflame, his essence like the sweetest poison that lingered in her veins. He could feel it in the way her eyes darkened when she looked at him—a look that said he wasn't just her lover—he was her addiction, her sustenance, the one thing she craved above all else.

As for the women—Camilla fed on their souls. While it didn't give her the vitality semen did, it was essential for her own demonic existence. Emiliano collected his trophies, and Camilla consumed her souls. It was a match made in hell.

When she finished, they curled up together in the front seat, sated and spent. The traveling, the sex, the bloodshed—it all left them exhausted. But their journey wasn't over yet. They still had a long road ahead to the hacienda.

Emiliano woke to find himself alone in the front seat. He glanced into the back, but all that remained was a mass of blood and torn body parts. Shaking off the fog of sleep, he stepped out, searching for Camilla.

Camilla emerged from the shadows, her every step a predatory glide. Blood glistened on her fingers, which she licked with slow, deliberate swipes of her tongue. Her eyes glowed with a dark, dangerous satisfaction—a wicked glow that spoke of the violent hunger she'd just quenched—and of the countless more she'd soon unleash. "Good morning, my love. Did you sleep well?" she purred.

Emiliano simply nodded, his gaze fixed on her bloody fingers.

Camilla smiled, amused. "Oh, this? I found myself a little breakfast. And I found us a new ride. Come on, my love," she said, extending her hand.

As they walked past a pile of blood-stained clothes, Camilla tossed him the keys to a car parked on the roadside. "All yours, daddy," she teased with a wicked grin.

They climbed into the stolen car and sped off, still heading toward that hacienda job Emiliano had heard about. The future promised more blood, more souls, and more of each other.

"He had expected her to scream,
to flee from the sight of the strange man
with his large cock still in hand,
blood smeared across his knuckles like a
twisted badge of honor."

CHAPTER 6
La Hacienda Aparicio

Driving down the secluded road, Emiliano couldn't help but revel in the utter isolation. The man on the phone had mentioned that the hacienda was remote, but this... this was perfect. The vast emptiness surrounding him fed his dark fantasies, and the thought of what he and Camilla could do in a place like this—unwatched, undisturbed—sent a thrill through him. He shifted in his seat, feeling the tightening in his pants. His fingers absently traced the outline of his growing erection as dark fantasies filled his mind, the pressure in his pants a delicious reminder of what awaited him.

A large, weathered sign loomed ahead, reading "La Hacienda Aparicio." Emiliano grinned. "We're here, amor," he said, his voice thick with anticipation. He reached over to grasp Camilla's hand, but she remained silent, staring at the hacienda as they approached. The silence between them was charged, filled with unspoken promises.

As they began the ascent up the winding road, Emiliano felt a strange excitement bubbling in his chest. When the massive hacienda finally appeared atop the hill, isolated and grand, it stole his breath. "You better disappear for a bit, my love. We can't have anyone seeing you with me." Camilla lingered, her gaze fixed on the hacienda, a silent, unreadable smile playing on her lips. Then, without a word, she dissolved into a puff of black mist.

Emiliano chuckled darkly. "Some small village is not going to know what hit them tonight," he murmured, parking the car. As he stepped out, the solitude of the place washed over him. No one for miles. Just him, Camilla, and their darkest desires.

He parked the car and stepped out, breathing in the crisp, clean air. The hacienda was everything he'd hoped for and more. It dominated the landscape, standing tall and proud against the sky, with no other signs of life in sight. Here, they could do whatever they pleased. The thought filled him with dark satisfaction.

He approached the heavy wooden door and knocked, the sound echoing through the stillness. When no one answered, he was about to knock again when he noticed an envelope tucked under the welcome mat. Curious, he bent down and retrieved it, noting the label: "Caretaker applicant." Scrawled across the front. Intrigued, he opened it.

The letter inside was straightforward, detailing the rules and conditions of the job.

Dear Applicant,

Welcome to La Hacienda Aparicio. We are pleased that you are interested in becoming our caretaker. Please be aware that a one-year contract must be signed, and during this time, you are not allowed to leave the property. Supplies will be delivered every six months, and the hacienda is currently stocked for the next six months. If you choose to accept the position, please dial 993 016 789 on the phone located in the entryway. Further instructions will be provided after you confirm your acceptance.

Warmest wishes, Management.

Emiliano's eyes gleamed as he read the letter. The conditions were strict, but they were exactly what he had hoped for—seclusion, privacy, and no interruptions. Camilla wasn't a person, after all. She was something else entirely. And as for visitors... well, they wouldn't be guests. They would be prey.

A dark chuckle escaped his lips as he stepped inside the hacienda. The air inside was cool and still, the kind of quiet that held secrets. The walls were a pristine white, contrasting sharply with the dark wooden beams that supported the vaulted ceilings. Sunlight streamed in through the large windows, casting long shadows across the terra cotta floors. The place was beautiful, but it had an undercurrent of something darker, something waiting.

His footsteps echoed as he crossed the room to the phone. Beside it was a notepad with a set of rules written in neat, precise handwriting:

1. You are not allowed to leave the property as long as you are under contract.

2. You are not allowed to have any guests or visitors during your time under contract.

3. You have full access to all of the grounds and every room, except for the main bedroom on the south side of the top floor. You are not to enter that room under any circumstance.

Once the contract is signed, it cannot be broken.

Emiliano smirked as he read the rules. They were easy enough to follow, especially with Camilla at his side. She wasn't a person, so technically, the rules didn't apply to her. And as for visitors... well, he had other plans for anyone who might stumble upon this place.

He picked up the phone and dialed the number, his heart pounding with anticipation. The line clicked, and a voice on the other end asked, "What is your answer?"

"I accept," Emiliano replied, his voice steady, full of dark promise.

"Your voice acts as a verbal contract agreement. The signed version will arrive with the next supply delivery in six months," the voice stated before abruptly hanging up.

Emiliano chuckled as he set the phone down. Not much for conversation, are they? He thought. But that was fine with him. He was here for other reasons.

He walked into the hacienda, the cool air of the interior washing over him. The bright white walls contrasted sharply with the dark beams overhead, creating a stark, almost sterile beauty. The terra cotta tiles underfoot were warm, familiar, but the gold-laid Saint Benedict crosses on each step of the spiral staircase seemed out of place—an unnecessary protection in a place that begged for sin.

Emiliano paused, running his fingers over the crosses, his touch almost reverent, before he ascended the stairs. They were built in a spiral design that allowed you to enjoy the beauty of the hacienda as you walked up the stairs. From the top, the view was breathtaking. The vast countryside stretched out before him, empty and waiting. But it was the hacienda itself that held his attention. This would be their playground, and there would be no limits to what they could do here.

The rooms were hidden at the back of the hacienda, secluded yet bathed in the same seductive glow as the rest of the estate. The terracotta tiles beneath Emiliano's feet felt warm, almost alive, as if they were welcoming him home. His fingers lingered on the thick, intricately carved wooden door, feeling the cool grooves of the craftsmanship. The door stood before him like a guardian—a beautiful yet imposing barrier between the present and the future he was so close to grasping.

He exhaled slowly, savoring the weight of the moment. With a soft, almost reverent creak, the door yielded to his touch, revealing the spacious room beyond. Sunlight poured in from the balcony, caressing the floor, the walls—an invitation to step into a world that was already his in all but name. The air held a faint trace of jasmine, mingling with the scent of polished wood and fresh linens, teasing his senses.

His gaze swept across the room, finally landing on the balcony. The view promised everything he craved: power, dominance, control. He could already picture Camilla standing there, her silhouette framed against the horizon, a queen surveying the kingdom they would soon rule. And with them, the helpless souls, they would bend to their will.

Soon, he thought, the word curling inside him like smoke. Very soon.

But it wasn't just the thrill of power that stirred within him. There was something else—a hunger that even Camilla might not fully understand. He couldn't wait to share it with her—this hunger, this insatiable need to consume and be consumed. And to see her unleash her own darkness, her own desires, upon those who would dare to challenge them.

The thought made his pulse quicken, a dark smile playing on his lips. Very soon, indeed.

The contrast between the pure white walls and the rich terracotta tiles was stark, almost startling. A massive canopy bed dominated the space, its ornate black curtains drawn back to showcase pristine white bedding. The twisted wrought-iron frame added a gothic touch that made Emiliano's breath catch in his throat. This room was a masterpiece—a perfect blend of elegance and darkness.

He wandered to the balcony, the cool mountain breeze greeting him like an old friend. Emiliano inhaled deeply, savoring the freshness of the air. Below, the hacienda grounds stretched endlessly. A large swimming pool sat at the center, its tiles mirroring the terracotta floor beneath his feet. The same gold Saint Benedict cross gleamed in the center, a strange and beautiful addition to the landscape. Beyond the pool, the trees marked the boundary of the vast countryside. Benches dotted the garden, inviting quiet reflection.

He couldn't help but imagine Camilla here, her beauty magnified by the surroundings. It was perfect—a sanctuary for their indulgences, far from the prying eyes of the world. He thought to himself how lucky he was to find a place like this for Camilla—lucky indeed.

But then, his fantasy was interrupted. In the distance, emerging from the tree line, was a woman. Her long, flowing blonde hair shimmered in the fading light. Her porcelain skin was almost glowing against the backdrop. She wore a sheer, white dress that clung to her body, revealing every curve. She was ethereal, like a ghost from a dream.

Emiliano froze, his gaze locked on her as she approached the pool. Without hesitation, she discarded the dress, letting it slip from her shoulders to the ground. Her nude form was flawless, each movement graceful and deliberate. She dove into the pool, cutting through the water with an ease that mesmerized him.

His pulse quickened. Every stroke, every kick of her legs sent ripples through the water and through him. He could feel himself growing hard, unable to look away. His hand instinctively moved to his pants, unzipping them as he watched her. The knife came out next, and with practiced ease, he sliced his palm. The blood dripped onto his erection, the sight and sensation sending a thrill through him.

He stroked himself, matching the rhythm of her swimming. The way her ass moved beneath the water, the soft bounce of her breasts as she floated on her back—it was all too much. He was lost in the moment, his breath heavy, his eyes glazed over with lust.

When he came, it was with a guttural groan that echoed across the grounds. His cum spilled from the balcony, and when he opened his eyes again, she was staring at him.

But there was no shock in her gaze, no fear—just a dark, knowing smile that made his heart stutter in his chest. He had expected her to scream, to flee from the sight of the strange man with his large cock still in hand, blood smeared across his knuckles like a twisted badge of honor. But instead of running, she swam to the edge of the pool, her movements fluid and predatory.

Her eyes locked onto Emiliano's, dark with an intensity that sent a shiver. directly through him. She spread her legs wide, a silent command rather than an invitation, her gaze never wavering as her hand moved to her breasts.

Her fingers teased her puffy nipples, rolling them slowly between her thumb and forefinger, drawing out her own pleasure as much as his torment. A soft gasp escaped her lips, a sound so faint yet filled with raw need that it sent a jolt straight to his core.

Emiliano's breath hitched as her other hand slid down, finding the swollen bud between her legs. She began to finger herself, her movements slow and deliberate, as if savoring every sensation. His eyes followed her every move, transfixed by the sight of her fingers working in rhythmic circles, moving in and out of her pussy, her body arching slightly in response.

He wanted to touch her, to claim her, but he was rooted in place, his hand finding his cock. Already hard and aching, he began stroking himself to her. The pull of her was irresistible, a force that demanded his complete surrender.

Her lips parted, a silent moan passing between them, a sound he could almost taste. The world around them faded away, leaving only the two of them in this heated, wordless exchange.

As their movements quickened, the tension between them coiled tighter, a shared rhythm building towards the inevitable. She watched him, her eyes gleaming with satisfaction, knowing she had him exactly where she wanted. Emiliano's grip tightened, his breathing ragged as he continued to stroke his cock, chasing the release that hovered just out of reach.

And then it happened. They came together, a silent eruption of pleasure that left him trembling, his body spent, his mind consumed by the intensity of the moment. She remained composed, a predatory smile curling her lips as her fingers traced slow, deliberate circles around her pussy, drawing out the last tremors of her ecstasy.

Emiliano's chest heaved, his gaze never leaving her, and in that moment, he knew he was lost to her, bound by a desire that went far beyond the physical. She was his torment and his salvation, and there was no escaping her.

He quickly pulled up his pants, his heart pounding in anticipation as he rushed downstairs. The allure of the mysterious woman had gripped him like a vice. He barely noticed the cool touch of the tiles under his feet as he flew down the stairs and out the back door, his gaze locked on the garden ahead. The pool sparkled under the sunlight, and there, at the far end, he could make out a hint of white. His breath quickened as he approached, his thoughts consumed by the woman who had captivated him.

But as he drew nearer, the white figure he'd been so eager to see revealed itself to be nothing more than a towel, caught on the edge of the pool. He froze, a chill creeping up his spine. Had he imagined it all? Was he hallucinating the entire encounter? His blood-stained and cum-soaked pants told a different story. The raw evidence of his recent experience clung to him, grounding him in reality yet leaving him more perplexed than ever.

He scanned the grounds, his eyes searching desperately for any sign of her. But there was nothing—no footsteps, no traces of anyone other than himself. The questions churned in his mind: Where had she gone?   Who was she? And why did she feel so real, only to vanish without a trace?

Frustration gnawed at him as he made his way back inside, retracing his steps to the bedroom where it had all begun. The silence of the hacienda seemed to mock him as he stepped out onto the balcony once more, his gaze sweeping the landscape. The pool, the garden, the hacienda itself—everything was the same, yet everything had changed. The white towel fluttered gently in the breeze, a cruel reminder of his disillusionment.

His arousal throbbed beneath his skin, his cock straining painfully against the tight confines of his pants. Frustration twisted inside him as he tried to make sense of the bizarre, encounter that still lingered in his mind. He shifted uncomfortably, adjusting himself with a low, irritated grunt, before turning away from the memory that refused to release him. Perhaps a distraction would help clear his head—anything to dispel the lingering heat she had left in her wake.

The hallway stretched out before him, long and dimly lit, the shadows playing tricks on his already troubled mind. He moved forward, opening each door he passed, Each room was a masterpiece of luxury, yet somehow, exactly alike, they felt hollow, devoid of life or purpose. The hacienda seemed to mock him with its perfection, offering no answers, only more questions.

His thoughts were consumed by the haunting image of her—the woman who had appeared so suddenly and vanished. just as quickly, leaving behind an intense, almost palpable connection that he couldn't understand. The memory of her soft skin, the way her lips had parted as if inviting him to claim them, sent a fresh wave of need through him, making it nearly impossible to focus on the task at hand.

At the end of the hall, was a large wooden door, thicker and more imposing than the rest. The Saint Benedict cross, cast in gleaming gold, stood proudly on its surface, almost daring him to enter. His fingers brushed over the cool, smooth wood, tracing the cross with a mix of reverence and defiance.

This was the room they had warned him about—the one forbidden to him. But Emiliano had never been one to shy away from danger or defy his own desires. Rules were for others to follow, not him. He pushed against the door and tested the lock with the sharp edge of his knife, but the door held firm, refusing to yield to his will.

A growl of frustration rumbled in his chest as he turned back, returning to the first bedroom. The need to act, to find answers, gnawed at him, but exhaustion weighed him down. With a sigh, he stripped off his clothes, letting them fall carelessly to the floor, and collapsed onto the bed.

The mattress welcomed him with a soft embrace, but his mind was far from restful. The woman's image lingered like a ghost at the edges of his consciousness, her mysterious allure an unsolved puzzle that drove him mad with desire and curiosity.

Sleep was a battle he slowly lost, sinking into its depths as the night wore on. But even in his dreams, she was there, a shadow he couldn't escape, her presence both a

torment and a comfort he didn't fully
understand.

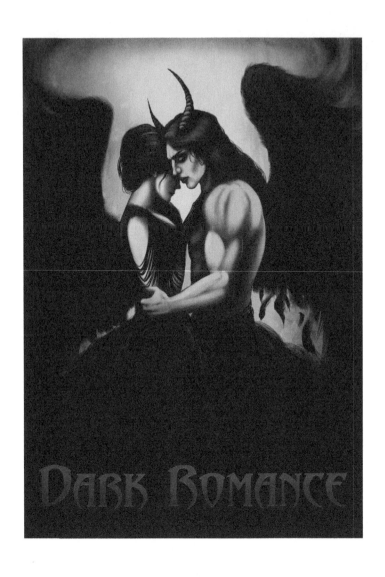

DARK ROMANCE

"Even in the grip of terror, the girl's body
betrayed her, her panties soaking wet,
her pussy wanting, her nipples hardening
painfully against the fabric."

CHAPTER 7

Dark Romance Girlie

A thick black mist crept through the streets, slithering like a living entity. It passed by buildings with open shades, pausing to peer inside, as if hunting for something—or someone. But it seemed as though nothing attracted its attention. It drifted along, unnoticed, until it reached a small, dimly lit coffee shop. Here, the mist paused, coiling at the threshold as if savoring the moment. Slowly, it began to descend, the air growing heavy with its presence. The black tendrils gathered at the ground, swirling and solidifying, until in their place stood Camilla.

She emerged from the darkness, her beauty a perfect blend of allure and danger, each curve a promise of pleasure and peril. Her lips curled into a seductive, knowing smile as she surveyed the empty shop, her presence commanding and otherworldly.

In the corner, a young woman sat engrossed in a book, oblivious to the world around her. Camilla's keen eyes noticed the title—one of those deliciously scandalous smut novels. She could smell her, the delicious aroma of her panties, feel the wetness between the woman's thighs, a physical manifestation of the dirty fantasies weaving through her mind. The slight parting of the girl's lips, the soft flush in her cheeks, the subtle shift of her thighs—every movement betrayed the excitement the words were sparking within her.

Camilla's body thrummed with anticipation; the thought of inflicting pain and pleasure with this girl sent shivers down her spine. A soft moan escaped her lips as she imagined the night that lay ahead, but a sudden prickling at the back of her neck warned her she was being watched.

Of course, she thought, turning her head slightly. Two young men leaned against a van outside, their eyes glued to her. Camilla smirked, letting them drink in the sight of her. She epitomized desire, and no one—especially not mere mortals—could resist her.

"This night just keeps getting better," she giggled to herself. Without breaking eye contact, she sauntered over to them, her hips swaying hypnotically. As she approached, she silenced any words they might have thought to utter with a single raised hand. "Before you try some pathetic line and ruin my mood, listen carefully. You're going to move this van over by the trees. Then I'm going to let you fuck me—both of you—as many times as you want. But here's the catch: don't disappoint me."

Her voice dropped to a dangerous growl, and the men, already ensnared by her glamour, had no choice but to obey. They scrambled into the van, drove it to a secluded spot, and eagerly opened the back doors, helping Camilla inside.

The van's interior was a den of depravity—ropes, duct tape, a bag meant for a head, plastic sheets lining the floor. They had planned to kidnap and brutalize some poor girl tonight, but those plans had changed. Camilla chuckled darkly. "Oh, you dirty little fucks! You were planning something wicked, weren't you? Too bad for you; Mama's in charge now."

She appraised them both, her gaze cold and calculating. Trying to figure out which one she wanted first. She was already turned on thinking about the girl in the coffee shop. "Strip," she commanded. They obeyed without hesitation, revealing toned bodies; neither impressed her—at least not by Emiliano's standards. But they would do for now.

Camilla's finger curled toward the smaller one, her eyes gleaming with predatory hunger. 'You. Crawl to me,' she purred. He crawled, each movement a silent plea for her favor, his body trembling under the weight of her gaze. When her lips met his, he felt the pull—an invisible thread winding tighter, siphoning his essence. His body crumbled inward, shrinking under the pressure of her hunger, until all that was left was a brittle shell, drained and discarded.

Camilla flicked the empty skin aside like a discarded garment, her gaze sliding to the remaining man, whose eyes widened with a mix of fear and arousal.

Impress me, or join him in oblivion,' she warned, her voice a silky threat as she leaned back against the van's cool metal. Her fingers danced over her skin like a promise of what was to come. The scent of the girl from the coffee shop lingered in her mind, driving her wild with lust.

"Now, come here and taste Mama's pussy," she ordered, her voice thick with desire.

The man crawled slowly to Camilla, and using his tongue, he began to lick her pussy with the urgency of a sinner seeking absolution, each flick a desperate prayer. Camilla's lashes quivered, the world fading as her mind conjured the girl's soft lips tracing lines of fire along her inner thighs. She envisioned the girl, her lips brushing against her most sensitive spots. The juices from her pussy drenching her thighs, the smell of sex and desire seeping from her pores.

Camilla's fingers found their way to her pussy, moving in time with the ragged cadence of her breath, her hips undulating in a slow, agonizing rhythm that begged for release. 'Deeper,' she commanded, her voice a low, dangerous growl, thick with unfulfilled hunger. His rhythm stuttered, and she felt his hesitation—a moment of weakness she refused to tolerate. Her nails dug into his scalp, guiding him with a force that brooked no argument.

Her tail slithered from the darkness, a serpent of cold, unyielding flesh coiling around his torso with possessive intent. With a soft rustle, her wings spread wide, shadows cascading from their edges as they clamped around his legs, trapping him in the storm of her desire.

"Deeper," she hissed, the words laced with a dark promise that sent a shiver down his spine. Her grip tightened, unforgiving, as her eyes gleamed with a malevolent hunger that brooked no defiance, only submission.

With a surge of dark energy, she drove his head deeper, using him with merciless precision, her body pulsing around him like a relentless tide, pulling him deeper with every thrust. " Like a living dildo, thrusting him in and out of her soaked pussy. "Yes, just like that, that's how Mama wants it, she moaned, her pace quickening as her climax approached. His body was buried up to his chest inside her pussy, her pleasure spiraled, a rising storm within her, until a roar of ecstasy tore from her lips, her black essence flooding around him in a torrent of dark release.

Panting, Camilla reclined, the remnants of her pleasure coursing through her like a lingering, bittersweet melody. "Nothing like a good orgasm to whet the appetite." A soft hum of satisfaction vibrated through her as her tail coiled, the tip slick with her cum, gliding gracefully toward her lips. She paused, letting the anticipation build, her eyes half-lidded with a mixture of hunger and pleasure. The taste flooded her senses, rich and intoxicating—a nectar she savored with a slow flick of her tongue. Her body shivered in response, the sweetness clinging to her like a dark promise, indulgent and forbidden, a taste that spoke of her power, her dominance over herself and anyone who dared challenge her.

Her victim squirmed in agony, his struggles weak and pitiful against the relentless force of her hunger. Camilla's inner muscles clenched, razor sharp teeth lining her pussy tearing through his flesh with a slow, merciless precision. Each moan that slipped from her lips mingled with the wet, grisly symphony of his demise, her pleasure rising in tandem with his despair, each bite, each gnash of teeth a testament to her unyielding dominance.

When her hunger was sated, she spat out his shoes with a soft, satisfied laugh, the remnants of his existence reduced to nothing more than discarded trinkets.

That was just a warm-up," she purred, a predatory glint sparking in her eyes as her mind drifted back to the girl. A slow, wicked smile curled her lips. "Let's see if my little bookworm can handle what's next.

Outside, the girl's fingers trembled slightly as she packed her things, the last sip of lukewarm coffee lingering on her tongue as she stepped into the shadowy embrace of the night. She had barely brushed past the rustling bushes when a hand clamped over her mouth, the harsh scent of leather filling her nostrils. Before she could scream, darkness swallowed her as a bag was yanked over her head. She thrashed wildly, her heart slamming against her ribs, but the arms around her were unyielding, lifting her off the ground as if she weighed nothing. The cold steel floor of the van bit into her skin as she was tossed inside, the world reduced to muffled sounds and her own rapid breathing.

Panic surged through her veins, a wild, primal terror that coiled in her gut. Yet beneath the fear, a darker pulse quickened—something forbidden, a thrill that fluttered low in her belly, betraying her in the most wicked way.

From the shadows, Camilla's gaze sharpened, the gleam in her eyes intensifying as she drank in the girl's subtle shifts—the quickened breath, the way her thighs pressed together in futile resistance. Even in the grip of terror, the girl's body betrayed her, her panties soaking wet, her pussy wanting, her nipples hardening painfully against the fabric.

A voice, rough and thick with dominance, rumbled in her ear, sending a shiver down her spine. "You'll do exactly as I say, or you'll wish you hadn't been born. Understand?" Her attempt to cry out died in her throat as a hand clamped around it, the pressure sharp and unyielding, silencing her into submission. "I said, do you understand?" His grip tightened, his breath hot against her skin, driving the command deeper. "What do you want with me?" She gasped, her voice trembling with fear and something more.

His free hand traced a slow, deliberate path up her thigh, fingertips grazing the damp heat that pooled there. "Look at you, dripping for me," he murmured, his voice a dark caress that sent a shock of shame through her. He brought his fingers to his lips, savoring the taste with a satisfied hum. "Sweet as sin."

"I'm going to let go now, but make a sound, and you'll regret it," he growled, each word a razor-sharp promise. He released her throat, only to drive his fingers deep inside her warm, wet pussy—a sudden invasion that stole her breath and replaced it with a strangled moan. Her hips bucked against his hand, helpless against the relentless rhythm. As he peeled the bag from her head, the dim light revealed his face—the cruel beauty of a predator sizing up his prey.

He loomed over her, a towering figure at six feet seven, his presence overwhelming in the dim light. Long, wavy hair tumbled across one side of his face, partially veiling a single blue eye that cut through her defenses like a blade. His body radiated strength, every sinew taut with power, a living embodiment of dominance.

"This is your last chance. Obey me, or suffer the consequences," he said, his voice low and menacing.

In a voice that resonated with authority, he commanded, "You will do everything I say, or else. Understand?"

Panic edged her voice as she cried out, "What do you want from me? Someone, please help!" His grip on her throat silenced her desperate pleas, firm yet measured enough to let her gasp for air.

"I told you; only do as I say! Not a single peep out of you!" he warned. Camilla could smell the dampness between her legs, arousal mixing with fear. She was getting off on this. As his grip loosened slightly, she cried out again, "Help, please someone help!" The hand tightened once more.

"You will learn to obey me!" he growled, tearing off her leggings and panties. Her arousal was evident, a traitorous moisture coating her thighs. His fingers traced a deliberate path up her quivering leg. "Fuck, baby girl, you taste delicious, he murmured, tasting her on his fingers. Her soft moan was both a surrender and a plea.

"I'm going to let go again," he growled, his voice low and dangerous, "but if you make a sound, I will punish you." His words were a dark promise that sent a shiver down her spine. Slowly, he released his grip and, in the same fluid motion, thrust two fingers into her soaked pussy, finger fucking her. His fingers moved with a commanding rhythm, each stroke drawing a gasp from her lips despite her efforts to stay silent. Her moans grew louder, a blend of defiance and submission, as the pressure inside her built.

Defiance flickered in her gaze; a wicked smile curled on her lips as she screamed 'Help!' once more, her voice trembling on the edge between fear and exhilaration."

"His grip tightened around her throat, eyes narrowing dangerously as he growled, 'You think this is a game?' His breath seared hot against her ear."

She shook her head, her eyes wide with fear and excitement. "No, Daddy," she whispered, her voice barely audible.

He unzipped his pants and revealed his large, thick cock. Her eyes widened in shock and awe, her body trembling with anticipation.

He shoved his thumb between her lips, and she began to suck on it, moaning softly. "You want Daddy's cock, don't you, baby girl?" He taunted, his voice dripping with sadistic pleasure.

She smiles softly as she stares at his huge cock, then slowly raises her gaze to meet his. "I want Daddy's cock," she pleads, her voice barely above a whisper.

He thrust his thick cock past her parted lips with a deliberate force, fingers tangling in her hair as he held her head firmly. His dominance was palpable; every movement was a command she was compelled to obey. She gagged slightly at his size, tears pricking her eyes as he filled her mouth completely.

The taste of him was intoxicating—an arousal-tinged blend of salt and musk that made her feel alive and wanted in a way she'd never experienced before. Each thrust sent ripples of heat through her body, igniting every nerve ending with electric anticipation.

In this moment, she was his to control, to mold to his desires, and the rawness of it thrilled her in ways she couldn't fully comprehend. His low growl reverberated through her core as she struggled to breathe around him, a primal sound that spoke volumes more than words ever could.

"I told you to keep quiet," he growled cruelly. "Let's see how much you can talk with my fat cock in your throat!" He laughed darkly as she willingly took him deeper, surrendering completely.

Her body shuddered with pleasure as he filled her entirely. "You like Daddy's cock?" he asked smugly. She moaned in affirmation, struggling to swallow him whole.

Abruptly, he pulls his cock out; she reached for him desperately, craving more. "You're going to be a lot of fun tonight," he said before throwing her onto her back and plunging into her soaking pussy effortlessly.

Wrapping his arms around her waist tightly, he began ramming into her harder and deeper with each thrust. Her moans grew louder until they became screams of ecstasy. "Fuck me, Daddy! Fuck me harder!" Her voice cracked under the weight of raw pleasure.

"I'm cuuuuummm..." was all she managed to say before climaxing around his relentless cock. He continued fucking her until finally cumming deep inside her.

Pulling out slowly, he leaned back in the van where they lay entangled moments ago—his still-twitching cock glistening with their combined juices—she stared at him longingly while pleasuring herself at the memory burning brightly in her mind.

The man transformed seamlessly into an ethereal beauty—the most captivating woman the girl had ever seen with an enchanting smile playing on her lips.

"Oh my little dark romance girlie," Camilla cooed tenderly. "You've been so much fun tonight—but we're not done yet."

I know your deepest cravings,' Camilla teased devilishly as a thick purple tentacle sprouted serpent-like from where a tail might have been—its pink suckers gleaming ominously under dim light.

"Well, actually...tentacles!" she corrected herself gleefully as multiple appendages slithered forth—the girl squealed in delight while continuing to finger herself frantically at the sight before being restrained by writhing tendrils that spread wide apart limbs helplessly.

"Fuck me!" she demanded breathlessly just before one tentacle slid down into her eager throat, filling it entirely as it writhed beneath her skin—all while another invaded both pussy and ass simultaneously —relentlessly fucking every available hole amidst moans mingled with pleasure-pain cries echoing through confined space within van confines...

Other tentacles wrapped themselves sensually around breasts—their suction cups working diligently upon sensitive nipples, eliciting further gasps from the captive audience below.

"Oh Emiliano, my love—I wish you were here—you'd adore how she tastes!" Camilla lamented, wistfully closing her eyes and briefly savoring the moment before cumming explosively through every invading appendage...

Dark black cum oozed forth, leaking uncontrollably from mouth-pussy-ass alike, leaving the girl sprawled and spent beneath a mere empty shell drained completely...

Camilla withdrew her tentacles, carefully surveying the aftermath, satisfied she—bestowed a final kiss upon lifeless lips, whispering a fond farewell... I'll never forget you, my little dark romance girlie.

Stepping out of the van cautiously, Camilla scanned her surroundings. Ensuring no witnesses lurked in shadows. Her lips curled into a sly smile as she approached the gas cap with deliberate slowness—a predator savoring her hunt's final moments. She snapped her fingers, conjuring a blue flame that danced hypnotically from her index finger. She inserted it into the gas tank, stretching it slowly until gasoline ignited, engulfing the entire van instantaneously in an inferno of passionate destruction.

She paused for a heartbeat, watching the flames consume their intimate playground. Her eyes reflected the flickering firelight as she savored every crackle and pop—a symphony of chaos that mirrored her unquenchable thirst for dominion.

She turned away from the blazing wreckage with an air of elegant detachment, each step fluid like liquid darkness against moonlit pavement. Thoughts of Emiliano whispered through her mind—his touch, his taste—filling her with a longing that was both bitter and intoxicating.

But tonight wasn't about him; it was about indulging in forbidden desires that left her lover spent beneath her exquisite control—a mere vessel drained completely by ecstasy's relentless demands.

Her fingers glided over her lips, still tingling from their final kiss—as she whispered tenderly into the night air:

"I'll never forget you, my little dark romance girlie. As shadows swallowed her form once more, Camilla vanished into obscurity—a haunting echo of sensuality left behind only for those daring enough to seek it out in whispered legends.

"Emiliano didn't stop,
drinking her in, his face wet
with her release as he licked her clean,
savoring every last drop."

CHAPTER 8

Our First Night

Slowly, Emiliano's eyes fluttered open, a groan escaping his lips as the soft, wet warmth enveloped his cock. Each gentle stroke sent ripples of pleasure through him as he moaned softly. He was certain it was Camilla, her touch unmistakable—until he glanced down. His breath caught in his throat.

Instead of his beloved, the deep blue eyes of the mysterious blonde woman stared back at him, gleaming with a mix of innocence and something darker. Emiliano's hand instinctively reached for her long, golden hair, gripping it gently, pulling her back just enough to watch her lips wrap around his shaft. Her gaze never wavered, locked onto his as she continued to pleasure him, each slow, deliberate stroke of her tongue bringing him closer to the edge. He wanted to say something, but his lips could only moan.

He was mesmerized by her. Who was she? What power did she hold over him?

Normally, he would have tightened his grip, forcing his cock deeper down her throat until she choked on it or stopped breathing, whichever came first. But this time, something held him back. His fingers, instead of strangling her, tenderly combed through her hair as she set the rhythm, her mouth wrapping around him like a vice of pure ecstasy.

She lifted her head, her lips releasing him with a soft pop before she crawled up his body. Emiliano's eyes followed her every move, her perfect breasts sliding up his torso, her hardened nipples grazing his skin. She leaned down, her lips brushing against his in a teasing lick, her deep blue eyes boring into him as though she could see straight through to his soul.

"Who are you?" He murmured against her lips but was silenced by her kiss, soft yet commanding, dissolving all conscious thought.

As she positioned herself over him, he could feel her heat and her wetness as she slid down onto his cock with an ease that made him shudder. He was big, almost too big for most women, but she took him in as though they were made for each other. Only Camilla had ever managed that before. His instincts screamed at him to grab her hips, to slam into her with a force that would leave her breathless, but again, something stopped him.

Instead, he let her set the pace, each slow descent tightening her around him like a vice, her pussy gripping his cock in a way that made his mind spin. His hands found her breasts, caressing them softly as she rode him, her moans only spurring him on. Emiliano's mouth sought out her nipple, his tongue swirling around the hardened peak before he sucked it into his mouth, her soft gasps echoing in his ears.

The confusion gnawed at him. He had never made love—never wanted to. But that was what this was. He didn't want to hurt her, to harm her, to take her life as he had done with so many others. His love for Camilla was born out of pain, their passion fueled by the suffering of others. But with this woman, all those dark cravings were gone. He felt...human for the first time in what felt like an eternity.

He wanted to ask her name to understand who she was and what spell she had cast over him, but as he opened his mouth to speak, she silenced him with a kiss. Her lips tasted of honey and sin, and he was lost in her, in the warmth of her body, in the sweetness of her touch.

She moved against him, their bodies entwined in a rhythm that felt both ancient and new, as though they had done this a thousand times before, and yet it was the first time. Emiliano felt her climax building—the tension in her body, the way her pussy clenched around him. His fingers tightened on her hips as he fought the urge to take control, to dominate her as he did with every other woman. To throw her on the bed and ram his cock into her ass. But he couldn't. He didn't want to.

Instead, he gently rolled her onto her back, spreading her legs wide as he kissed his way down her body, savoring the taste of her skin and the scent of her arousal. His breath ghosted over her pussy, and she moaned, the sound shooting straight to his cock. He paused, inhaling deeply, her scent intoxicating. Then, slowly, he began to taste her, licking along her folds, savoring every drop of her essence. Her taste was unlike anything he had ever experienced—sweet, addictive, and he wanted more.

His tongue danced over her clit, his thumb rubbing in slow, deliberate circles as he brought her closer and closer to the edge. He inserted two fingers inside her, curling them just right, feeling her walls tighten around him as she came, her body shuddering with the force of it. Emiliano didn't stop, drinking her in, his face wet with her release as he licked her clean, savoring every last drop.

He kneeled between her legs, sliding his cock back inside her, the heat of her pussy wrapping around him like a glove. His strokes were slow, deliberate, as he wiped his face clean with his fingers, sucking her cum from them one by one. Leaning down, he locked his hands with hers, kissing her deeply, letting her taste herself on his lips as they continued to make love. For the first time, there was no anger, no need to dominate or destroy. Only the overwhelming desire to be close to her, to feel her body against his, to be one with her.

The feelings terrified him. Emiliano had never known fear—until now. And what he feared most was the beauty of what they were doing—the love he was starting to feel.

They made love for what seemed like hours, lost in each other, in the pleasure, in the connection that seemed to go beyond the physical. Emiliano felt his climax approaching; he kissed her deeply as he came inside her, the release more powerful than anything he had ever felt before. He didn't want it to end; he didn't want to let her go as he held her tightly, kissing her with a passion that left them both breathless.

"When his eyes finally fluttered open, emptiness greeted him. The lingering ache of her absence throbbed through him, his cock tingling with the phantom traces of their connection—too vivid to dismiss as a mere dream. Yet she was gone, as elusive as smoke slipping through his fingers. Madness whispered in the void she left behind. A noise from the balcony drew his attention, and the doors flew open, a thick black mist rolling in. His heart leaped as he recognized the familiar presence. Camilla had returned.

The mist coalesced into a form, her demonic features slowly taking shape. Large black wings with deep red veins spread out behind her, her body covered in scales that gleamed in the moonlight. Her hands ended in sharp talons, and her lips, dark as night, parted to reveal fangs that gleamed in the darkness. Her long black hair framed her face, draping over her shoulders, while two curved horns arched gracefully above her head, completing her terrifying yet beautiful appearance.

"I'm back, my love. I missed you tonight," Camilla hissed, her voice a seductive purr as she glanced at herself in the mirror. "I'm sorry, my love. I forgot I was in my true form. Is this better?"

Before his eyes, her scales melted away, replaced by the smooth, bronzed skin of her human guise. Her horns retracted, becoming thick, luxurious black hair that cascaded down her back. A tight red dress hugged her curves, accentuating every inch of her perfect body as she strutted towards him, her hips swaying seductively.

"You're beautiful in every form, Mi Reina! All I ever see is stunning beauty," Emiliano replied, his voice thick with desire. His eyes fell to his own body, noting the renewed hardness of his cock. Camilla's gaze followed, a wicked smile spreading across her lips.

"I see you're ready for me," she purred, crawling onto the bed, her snake-like tongue darting out to wrap around his cock. She took him deep into her throat, the sensation almost too much for him to bear as her tongue stroked him, her throat tightening.

Camilla, the embodiment of hunger incarnate, was no ordinary lover—her very essence thrived on the vitality she drew from men, a succubus whose need knew no bounds. Even after Emiliano's release, her thirst remained unquenched, her relentless mouth and hands drawing him past the edge of exhaustion, claiming every last drop until he lay spent, a husk in her embrace.

With his final release, exhaustion claimed him. Camilla licked him clean, curling up against him, her body wrapping around his as he drifted off into a deep, dreamless sleep.

Their connection was unbreakable, forged in the fires of hell and sealed with the blood of their victims. Nothing could tear them apart—except death, and even that was a challenge Camilla would never allow.

"But Emiliano, there is goodness within you.
Allow me to awaken it.
Do not reveal my existence to her.
Keep this secret until
we can sever her hold over you.
I am forever yours; find me in your dreams until
we can be together."

CHAPTER 9

Elena

Emiliano woke alone, the other side of the bed cold and empty. He'd slept soundly, yet the vision of a beautiful blonde woman haunted his dreams, calling to him with a voice that felt hauntingly familiar. Rising, he wandered naked to the balcony, his eyes scanning the horizon for any sign of Camilla. She was nowhere to be seen—likely stirring trouble in a nearby village, he smirked at the thought—perhaps she'd bring back a new 'toy' for them to play with.

The image of the blonde refused to fade, compelling him towards a locked door at the hacienda's far end. As he approached, her scent enveloped him—a captivating aroma that he could only associate with her essence. It filled the air, thick and inviting. She was here, hidden behind this door, but why?

"Who are you," he murmured under his breath, as though saying her name might conjure her from behind that wooden barrier.

He knocked softly at first, then harder with each unanswered plea until his fists throbbed with pain.

"I don't know if you're behind this door," he started, his voice a raw whisper, "but I can't escape the thought of you. My name is Emiliano, and "I am not a good man by any measure. I've committed horrors beyond imagining." His voice faltered before it gathered strength again. "Yet your kiss dispelled my darkest thoughts. It's a rarity for someone as pure as you to dare to reach out to a soul as damned as mine. To see the light, one must appreciate the dark; I was born into it, molded by it. And yet, your light managed to pierce through, offering a glimmer of something different—redeemment, perhaps. My mind, my heart, and

My very soul is diseased and damaged, but your kiss suggested they might yet be mended. Perhaps now you wish to flee, knowing the depth of my darkness. But I had to reveal my heart to you. Can you envision a life with me? Is there a chance for us?"

No answer came. He rose slowly, his heart sinking with each silent moment. As he started to walk away, a slip of paper fluttered under the door. It was aged, the edges torn, the craftsmanship exquisite, bearing a message in deep crimson ink:

Dearest Emiliano,

Do not see your darkness as a barrier but as the very force that drew me to you. We all bear scars; we all seek what may mend us. True darkness, my dear, is not the mere absence of light but the refusal to see it. And you, Emiliano, are stepping towards the light by seeking me. Darkness cannot drive out darkness; only light can. It isn't you who forged this shadow—it's Camilla. A succubus, thriving not just on human essence but nurturing the darkest parts of you. She is a succubus, and she can only survive on the seed of males or on the souls of humans. She has fed on you year after year; the both of you are now joined. She feeds your darkness. She feeds the deeds that you are not proud of.

She keeps you hidden in the darkness. To be free, to be truly with me, you must release her hold on you.

Remember, only in your dreams can you find me until we can be together without shadows between us.

Your Elena

Emiliano slipped the letter into his pocket, his fist pounding the door once more, yearning for it to yield. "Elena, my love, why won't you open the door? You inhabit my thoughts and my heart; why can't my arms hold you too?" His voice, laced with desperation and love, echoed in the silent hallway. "In your embrace, I found a light that warmed my soul. Our lips met, and love surged through me, washing away the hate and pain that usually courses through my veins."

He paused, his heart torn. "How can I turn away from Camilla? She has been my savior, my protector, all these years. She loves me for who I am, fostering my darkest thoughts without fear. As much as I yearn for you, pushing Camilla away seems impossible," he confessed to the unyielding door.

The silence that followed was suffocating. Emiliano strained to hear a whisper, a breath from Elena—anything to persuade him to choose her. But the silence remained unbroken, and he slumped in defeat.

Then, a rustle—a note—slipped through the door.

My love Emiliano,

Camilla has deceived you. She didn't save you; she ensnared you. Consider who turned your family against you. She glamoured them into beating you, molesting you, and abusing you. She orchestrated that horrendous night at the barn, whispering the idea to invite all those sexual predators, ensuring your soul was tormented and sold. It was only when your rage and hatred coursed through your veins as you were being sodomized over and over that she intervened, manipulating your thoughts

towards vengeance and empowering you to enact it.

She glamoured you and fed you the thought of revenge and murder and then gave you the strength to kill everyone in that barn.

She hasn't nurtured your true self; she crafted the person you are. But Emiliano, there is goodness within you. Allow me to awaken it. Do not reveal my existence to her. Keep this secret until we can sever her hold over you. I am forever yours; find me in your dreams until we can be together.

Forever yours, Elena.

Emiliano's mind raced. Could this be true? Was his identity a fabrication by Camilla's design? He vividly recalled the brutality of that night—the laughter and scorn, the cold touch of many hands. He saw again the beautiful figure approaching him, the knife in her hand, the kiss that gave him the strength to exact his revenge. If Camilla had crafted his darkest desires, what was left of him that was truly his own?

If she was the one that created him, did it even matter? She loved him. Camilla was the only one that knew his dark heart and what it desired. And no matter how sadistic his cravings were, she was always there to assist him.

He was torn, his loyalty to Camilla warring with the newfound hope Elena offered. Sitting in the garden, he gazed out at the rolling Spanish countryside, lost in thought, wondering if the light Elena promised could ever truly illuminate his darkness.

"With predatory efficiency, Camilla's eyes turned
jet-black as she bit down hard on his cock.
She drank deeply from the open wound
as his lifeforce faded away into a hollow shell of
flesh and bone."

CHAPTER 10

Soledad

Camilla sensed an unsettling shift in Emiliano's usual unshakeable demeanor; his confidence seemed fractured since their arrival. An anomaly she couldn't ignore since they arrived in this secluded paradise. Despite her own dark desires, seeing Emiliano like this stirred a rare form of concern within her.

She knew what would restore that glint of assuredness in his eyes—a new addition to their ever-growing collection of playthings. With a resolve as dark as her soul, she woke before dawn, slipping away while Emiliano still slumbered, haunted by dreams he'd never share.

Camilla transformed into a black mist, soaring over the lush countryside, her dark soul still appreciating its beauty.

Below, a couple shared a heated embrace by the water's edge. The man's skilled hands wandered beneath the woman's dress, her breaths quick and deep—Camilla knew he was adept at pleasure. But he would serve as merely a distraction, the woman, a pristine offering for Emiliano.

Camilla desired a fresh pussy for her lover, so she discreetly flew behind some bushes. As the man deepened their kiss, Camilla whispered seductively in a tone only a male could hear, planting thoughts in his mind about needing to find a private spot to relieve himself. Confused yet compelled, he removed his hand from under her dress, "No! Don't stop... I'm so close!" the woman cried out in frustration as he pulled away abruptly.

"I'm sorry, my Soledad. I'll be back soon; I need to go relive myself, and then I'll fuck you," he promised before disappearing behind some bushes.

His breath caught when he stepped into a secluded grove, eyes narrowing as he caught sight of an ethereal figure shrouded in mist.

He had seen beauty before—Soledad was renowned as the village's enchantress—but this vision far surpassed earthly allure.   She was an intoxicating apparition, a siren calling him deeper into forbidden waters. His heart pounded as he took in every detail hungrily.

Her long black hair clung to her glistening skin, cascading down her back like midnight silk. Each movement she made sent ripples through the water that accentuated the lush curves of her hips and ass—a symphony that played solely for him. He felt his pulse quicken, a primal hunger stirring within him.

As she gracefully turned, pouring water over her raven locks, he marveled at the perfection of her form—the generous swell of her breasts taut against her chest with each breath she took—a vision sculpted by gods.

Camilla knew he was watching her. This was all part of her plan. She turned slowly, pretending to be surprised by his presence.

His throat tightened; desire mixed with urgency coursing through his veins. He wanted—no needed—to possess this creature who seemed almost too exquisite for mortal touch.

"Who are you?" The words slipped past his lips involuntarily, barely louder than a whisper yet heavy with intent.

She glanced over her shoulder towards him, eyes meeting his with an intensity that sent shivers down his spine, powerful, commanding yet inscrutably calm.

"Do you wish to find out?" she asked softly, her voice dripping with seduction and hidden challenges.

This small exchange hung in the air between them like an unspoken pact as he took a step closer, compelled by forces. beyond reason or morality—his desire overshadowing every other thought.

As Camilla began caressing her own flesh, she saw the man's desire morph into raw need. She moaned softly, letting every sound pull him deeper into her web of seduction. She pinched her nipples as she softly bit her lip, letting him know just how much she loved it. The delicious pain sent shivers through her body, intertwining with an overwhelming sense of surrender.

Her hand slowly traced downwards, fingers moving with agonizing slowness over every inch of her skin until they reached her pussy. She reveled in each brush against her sensitive flesh, teasing herself until she couldn't bear it any longer. She began to finger herself as soft moans escaped her lips, never breaking eye contact with him.

Each step closer was deliberate torture—an art form she'd perfected over centuries. When she finally stood before him, she could see the raw lust in his eyes. A testament to her influence. Leaning close, her breath a whisper of promises that flirted with the line between cruelty and ecstasy, she traced her fingers along her own moistened lips, her soft moans filling the space between them.

With deliberate sensuality, she fingered herself, her moans echoing in his ears, amplifying his desire. Slowly, she drew her glistening fingers up to his lips, offering a taste of her essence. He accepted eagerly, his lips closing around her fingers, savoring the sweetness that he likened to the nectar of the gods, its aroma as heady as the most exquisite wine.

Camilla kneeled before him, her dark eyes locking onto his with an intensity that bordered on obsession. She unzipped his pants with deliberate slowness, maintaining eye contact as she began a sensual stroke of his already hard cock.

I'm going to make you feel so good, baby," she whispered, her voice a silky caress. "Let Mama do what she knows best."

As he closed his eyes and tilted his head back, lost in the rising wave of sensations, Camilla's demon tongue slipped out. It coiled around his length like a possessive serpent, pulling him deep into her throat. His legs trembled under the unparalleled pleasure; no mortal woman could compare.

As he felt himself cumming, he grasped her head firmly, ensuring she would take every drop. As he started to cum, he pushed her deeper onto his cock, exploding down her throat with fervor. But as he tried to withdraw, she tightened her grip and sucked harder. His body betrayed him, another surge emptying into her relentless mouth.

Desperation set in as he tried to push away—a futile effort against her supernatural strength.   Her hands gripped his ass with claws that formed mid-embrace, anchoring him in place. As panic threatened to overtake pleasure, her tail snaked up and forced its way into his mouth, muffling any cries for mercy.

She continued her relentless assault until there was nothing left for him to give. Euphoric from his depletion, Camilla's own climax came violently down his throat—a dark substance coating his insides like ink spreading through water.

With predatory efficiency, Camilla's eyes turned jet-black as she bit down hard on his cock. She drank deeply from the open wound as his lifeforce faded away into a hollow shell of flesh and bone.

Satisfied, Camilla discarded what remained in the water, watching it drift away. She then composed herself and approached Soledad, who was lost in her own pleasure, eagerly awaiting the return of her lover, a reunion that would never come.

Camilla hissed softly as she approached Soledad, her form now eerily resembling the man she had just consumed. "Soledad," she murmured, her voice dripping with venomous allure, "You are the perfect gift for my love." Her eyes glinted with dark promise as she added almost nonchalantly, "But first... I need my own little taste."

Camilla tore away Soledad's clothes, savoring every inch of exposed skin like a predator stalking its prey. Her breasts were large but perfectly shaped, and her hips were thick and wide. Soledad shivered under her gaze—thick curves that beckoned like forbidden fruit—ripe with sensuality yet tinged with an undercurrent of fear.

"Emiliano will adore his plaything," Camilla mused silently as she watched Soledad kneel before her grabbing the man's cock, unsuspecting that it was Camilla's serpentine tail. As Soledad took it into her mouth, Camilla's lips curled into a satisfied smirk—letting her suckle while eyes gleamed with both hunger and restraint.

The urge to take what she wanted surged through Camilla like wildfire, an all-consuming craving that ignited her very core. Yet she tempered this primal hunger with caution; Emiliano's pleasure was paramount, and she dared not damage his exquisite toy. Soledad's beauty was undeniable—delicate features framed by cascading dark hair—but her inexperience was evident in every clumsy movement of her lips around Camilla's cock.

Camilla's eyes gleamed with a mix of lust and condescension as she watched Soledad struggle. 'Not like that,' she murmured under her breath, a barely audible directive laced with authority. She stepped closer, her presence imposing yet intoxicating.

'Watch and learn,' Camilla whispered harshly as she crouched next to Soledad, her fingers threading through the younger woman's hair, guiding her rhythm with calculated precision. The air seemed to pulsate with the raw energy of dominance and submission.

Camilla reveled in the power coursing through her veins—the thrill of control over both Emiliano's pleasure and Soledad's education. Her senses were heightened; every gasp from her lips, every shudder from Soledad resonated deep within her."

She abruptly pulled Soledad away, spinning her around onto all fours—a position that bespoke both vulnerability and eager anticipation. Camilla's fingers trailed up Soledad's spine, each touch leaving a shiver in its wake. She knew Emiliano rarely did anal; this forbidden territory was all for Camilla tonight.

"You're mine tonight," she whispered huskily into Soledad's ear.

With calculated forcefulness, Camilla's thick tail-cock slid deep into Soledad's ass—a sharp squeal escaping from those parted lips, but as Camilla expected, this little whore loved it.

Soledad's senses were overwhelmed; every nerve ending seemed to spark alive. under Camilla's dominance. Her own mind battled between resistance and yielding completely to this dark ecstasy.

"You're going to love this," Camilla murmured, her voice velvet-soft yet edged with steel as she gripped Soledad's thick hips tighter. Each thrust was a measured act of dominance, filling Soledad in ways she'd never been before. The air was filled with the symphony of their bodies meeting—wet sounds mingling with desperate moans that only drove Camilla further into madness.

With every stroke deeper than the last, Camilla felt an intoxicating sense of control wash over her—a stark contrast to the chaos outside these walls. Her fingers dug into Soledad's supple flesh, feeling every quiver that rippled through her lover's body.

Soledad's breath hitched with each impactful thrust. She felt herself unraveling under Camilla's relentless rhythm, each movement sending waves of pleasure crashing through her. Her back arched involuntarily as she tried to meet every powerful stroke.

"Beg for it," Camilla commanded, tightening her grip until her nails left crescent moons on Soledad's skin.

"Please," Soledad whimpered between gasps, each word laced with overwhelming need as she surrendered completely to Camilla's control.

Each thrust sent waves of ecstasy rippling through them—a carnal symphony punctuated by the relentless rhythm of flesh meeting flesh. Soledad's breath came in ragged gasps as her body responded eagerly, her ass clenching around Camilla's tail-cock with each powerful stroke.

Soledad could feel the climax unfurling within her like a slow-burning fuse, each thrust winding tighter until she teetered on the brink of release. Her moans escalated into desperate pleas, her voice raw with need.

"I said fucking beg for it," Camilla hissed, her voice dripping with dark authority as she maintained her punishing rhythm.

Soledad's nails clawed at the damp grass beneath her; she was on the edge, she felt herself about to cum, but her body craved even more from Camilla's fierce dominance. "Please fuck me harder," she gasped out, every word trembling with pent-up desire and complete submission.

The admission seemed to satisfy Camilla, whose own breath hitched in response. She drove deeper with renewed intensity, pushing Soledad over the edge. As Soledad's climax tore through her, she screamed a primal sound of pure, unadulterated pleasure that echoed through the air.

Soledad began to cum again from the relentless ass fucking she was getting; just feeling her ass tighten around Camilla's tail-cock pushed Camilla over her own edge. She came deep within Soledad's ass, filling her up with hot cum that overflowed when she pulled out.

Bending down without hesitation, Camilla licked up every drip of the black cum that leaked out with a wicked smile gracing her lips. "Fuck, I taste amazing!" she murmured, voice tinged with triumph and satisfaction.

By now, Soledad was under Camilla's glamouring spell. She stood up mechanically, arms outstretched like a puppet on invisible strings.

Camilla took a step back and transformed into her demon form—an awe-inspiring metamorphosis that made her simultaneously terrifying and mesmerizing. Her wings unfurled to an impressive twenty-foot span while her hands and feet sharpened into lethal talons. Her skin turned a seductive shade of deep crimson, contrasted by her midnight-black wings, tail, and claws. Dark black horns crowned her flowing hair, retaining the silky texture that had once been comforting but now seemed sinister.

Hovering effortlessly above Soledad, Camilla clasped her shoulders with clawed feet before lifting off towards the hacienda with confidence born from knowing she was unseen in this desolate hour.

Her large black wings glided her through the air as she approached the garden bathed in moonlight. She placed Soledad opposite from the pool, ensuring Emiliano would have an unobstructed view of her. As she landed softly behind Soledad, her wings folded seamlessly into her back, transforming her back into her human form.

Emiliano was deep in sleep when a vivid dream took hold—a vision of Elena materialized at the foot of his bed, completely naked. "Fuck me, Emiliano," she whispered huskily as she began touching herself provocatively. "I want to feel your cock inside me!" She crawled onto the bed slowly, delicately drawing out his massive cock before licking its head teasingly and sucking on the tip.

Even in his dream state, Emiliano felt a familiar urge—an insatiable desire to dominate completely, to choke her and shove her hard on his cock—but some unseen force always held him back with Elena, she was different; with her, he couldn't unleash himself fully. Just as she began choking on his girth in surprise, she vanished into darkness.

From the void, Camilla's commanding presence materialized, her voice a soft yet firm summon. "Come to me, my love," she called. "I have brought you a gift."

Emiliano's eyes fluttered open as he instinctively moved toward the balcony. Below him stood Camilla, her wings partially unfurled behind a beautiful naked woman whose large breasts were already drawing a lustful grin from him.

The lingering frustration from his restraint with Elena simmered within him. He yanked off his clothes and dashed outside; his cock slapped against his thighs as he approached them.

His hands traced Soledad's body tenderly at first, escalating in fervor as he fondled her breasts more roughly. Thank you, my love. "You always know what I need," he whispered to Camilla before pressing his lips against hers.

"Show me," Camilla purred from behind him as she let her wings envelop Soledad's arms and legs, spreading them invitingly for Emiliano. Fuck her, my love! Camilla groaned. Her wings reached over Emiliano and held Soledad up by her arms while she spread Soledad's legs wide apart.

Emiliano's heart pounded as he grabbed his large cock and teased it against Soledad's slick entrance. Her pussy looked so tight it made him burn hotter with need. "Here is some lube, my love!" Camilla said as she raked her claws across Soledad's belly. Blood welled up from the scratches, its metallic scent mingling with the floral notes of her perfume—a heady mixture that drove him wild.

As blood dripped from Soledad's wounds, Emiliano felt an intoxicating surge of power course through him. He rubbed his hands in her blood, coating his cock until it glistened darkly under the dim light. With deliberate slowness, he slid two fingers inside her tight pussy to prepare her for what was coming next.

She's perfect for you," Camilla whispered close to his ear, her breath hot against his skin as she watched intently. "Look at how she trembles.

Taking more blood, Emiliano smeared it across Soledad's large tits and swollen nipples before leaning down to lick it off hungrily. The taste of copper fueled his lust even further as he rammed his fat cock deep inside her without warning.

Soledad let out a deep groan that echoed through the air as she felt every inch of Emiliano's massive cock stretching her insides. Each thrust brought a new wave of pleasure and pain that left them both gasping for more.

"Harder!" Camilla demanded with sadistic glee as she kneeled before Soledad's quivering form, extending her demon tongue to circle around those perfect dark nipples that had captivated Emiliano so utterly.

Look how they respond," Camilla cooed. "They're perfect for your collection." Her name is Soledad, and she's all yours.

Her words spurred him on—he clamped onto Soledad's thick hips and drove himself harder into her body until he exploded inside her with a guttural roar.

Camilla's hunger went beyond mere satisfaction; she craved the reinstatement of their dark, twisted symphony. 'Don't stop! Keep fucking her,' she commanded, her voice a sultry whisper dripping with authority. Sliding behind him once more, she emitted a low growl of encouragement as her hands traced possessive paths along his thighs.

Her breath was hot against his skin as she took one of his balls into her mouth, flicking her tongue with deliberate precision before trailing lower, exploring forbidden territory. She could feel him tense as her tongue danced at the entrance of his ass, teasing before plunging inside with a wicked intent. Each flick, each thrust of her tongue in his ass sent shivers up his spine. There was something primal about the way his body responded, hips bucking forward as he thrust deeper into Soledad.

Emiliano's grip on reality teetered as he felt himself about to cum again the surge building within him once more. His thighs tensed involuntarily as he released deep inside Soledad again, a deep growl escaping his lips. Camilla circled around them like a predator closing in on its prey, her hands finding Soledad's breasts with possessive force.

"Now take your prize, my love," she commanded with a voice that dripped authority and seduction. "Take what is yours!"

Emiliano's eyes glowed with dark desire as he leaned forward slowly. The moment was thick with anticipation before his teeth sank into Soledad's nipple with brutal finality. He savored the coppery tang of her blood on his tongue while his hands coiled around her throat like twin vipers.

The air seemed to hold its breath as Emiliano choked her with unrelenting strength, feeling the life fade away beneath his grip. His thrusts became more frenzied as her body went limp in his hands, turning lifelessness into his ultimate aphrodisiac. It was at this pinnacle of depravity that he found release—exploding inside her with an intensity that left him breathless and spent.

Pulling away with a smirk, Emiliano placed Soledad's severed nipple inside the silken bag Camilla handed him. He savored the coppery taste lingering on his lips before sealing the bag and labeling it "Soledad."

He turned back to Soledad's lifeless body sprawled on the ground. His eyes were drawn to Camilla, who was hungrily sucking his cum from Soledad's pussy. Her demon tongue flicked deep inside, desperate for every last drop. If she acted quickly enough, she could still swallow Soledad's soul before it escaped into the ether. Emiliano was mesmerized as he watched Camilla draw the essence from Soledad through her pussy.

His tongue traced his lips again; he could still taste Soledad's flesh. Glancing up toward the hacienda, he saw Elena on the balcony. Her eyes bore into his soul. Though he yearned to call out or signal her, he was paralyzed; no words or sound could leave his mouth. She simply turned away and disappeared into the shadows of the hacienda.

Just as he resolved to go after her, Camilla's lips enveloped his still-hard cock with an insatiable hunger. She ensured that no drop of their dark ritual went unfelt.

Standing up gracefully yet seductively, she pressed a kiss to his lips. "I am always here for you, my love," she whispered seductively in his ear, her breath warm and intoxicating. "You are mine, and I am yours forever! Our love is a dark, twisted melody that echoes through eternity between our souls."

"Now go rest," she commanded softly but firmly while picking up what remained of Soledad's body. With a flourish of her wings, she ascended into the night sky.

Emiliano watched until Camilla disappeared from view before turning back toward the hacienda. Confusion gnawed at him like a ravenous beast. He relished taking lives and collecting trophies—a ritualistic homage to his darker desires. But when he was with Elena, those urges were subdued by an inexplicable serenity.

Why couldn't he have both? He pondered this forbidden thought even though he knew it was impossible. Camilla would never tolerate another unless they were left lifeless after their playtime. And Elena had already made it clear—Camilla had to be gone.

He trudged slowly back to the hacienda with a heavy heart and mind full of tumultuous thoughts.

"That's how we will fuck when we're alone,"
she declared softly but firmly.
"Only when I know you are fully mine can you do
anything you want with my body.
Get rid of Camilla!"

CHAPTER 11

Memento Dolor

Camilla had been gone awhile as Emiliano lay on the bed staring at the ceiling, haunted by visions of Elena watching Camilla suck him off from the balcony. Knowing she had seen them degrade that worthless human gnawed at him. Would she still want him? Could she look at him the same way? Questions whirled through his mind like dark shadows.

He sprung from the bed and ran down the hall to Elena's room, pounding on the large wooden door until its echoes filled every corner of the hacienda.

"Elena," he whispered hoarsely through the door. "Please come out and see me! I'm sorry you had to see that... I know you don't want me to be like this... But these cravings... they don't leave easily." His voice cracked with desperation. "Being bathed in darkness and evil, one's entire life doesn't wash off quickly. But when I am with you...

those cravings are subdued." He pressed his forehead against the door, closing his eyes. "I don't ever wish to hurt you; I only want to love you—to satisfy you. To touch your beautiful porcelain skin... embrace your beauty with all my senses." He paused, breathless. "Perire est mori—to lose your beauty would be death!"

Silence reigned throughout the villa; even nature held its breath. All he could hear was his own heartbeat pounding in sync with his frantic thoughts. Emiliano just sat there with his head hung between his knees, a posture betraying both defeat and latent fury. His fingers clenched into fists against his thighs, nails digging painfully into flesh as if physical pain could drown out the turmoil within.

Finally, a rustle broke through—the soft sound of paper sliding under the door. He looked down at the antique parchment. It was the same as before. Picking it up to see what Elena had written.

My Emiliano,

I see you know Latin, my love. Well, then you should know this. Amor est dolor! Remember that, my love, because love is pain. The pain you feel in your heart when you realize how much you love someone. The pain you feel when you know there is something keeping you apart. And the worst of all, the pain of losing that love. Remember that pain because the cure is in your hands. I am here for you, and my body is yours. You know what stands between us and what has to be done. I know who you are, my love. I know what lurks in the dark corners of your heart and soul. I know what the shadows whisper for you to do. But together we can make that go away. You must get rid of Camilla for any of this to work.

Emiliano let the note slip from his hand as if it burned him. Frozen in place, words failed him completely.

Slowly rising back up, he faced that formidable door again.

"My love," he murmured brokenly against it once more before straightening himself, finally facing head on towards that large portal, sealing away everything important inside there, including their future together, now threatened so gravely...

Camilla is not easy to get rid of," Emillíano mused, his voice a sultry whisper that seemed to caress the shadows dancing on the walls. "You know she is a succubus, but you may not know her true power. Even I am not fully aware of her strengths."

"But I do know she is not a lower-level demon," he continued, his eyes darkening with unspoken fears. "And the moment she discovers you, well, us... her wrath will be unstoppable." His voice trembled, slightly, betraying his deep-seated anxiety.

He leaned against the doorframe, feeling the cool wood press against his back as he waited for her response. He knew it would come in the form of one of her elusive letters. His heart pounded in his chest, each beat echoing through the quiet room like a drum of doom.

How can I protect you if I can never see you outside of your room? Each time we make love, you vanish as quickly as you appeared," he murmured softly to himself, reminiscing about your fleeting touch that left him yearning for more. The memories were bittersweet—intoxicating yet torturous.

Just as expected, a letter slid beneath the door once more—a lifeline tethering him to her amidst this storm of chaos. His hands shook slightly as he reached down to retrieve it, anticipation and dread coiling within him like twin serpents ready to strike.

He unfolded the parchment carefully; it was her handwriting—delicate strokes that promised both salvation and damnation.

My Love,

There is no need for concern on your behalf; I lack the strength to and power to defeat Camilla—only you can do that. But surely you've noticed the symbols adorning the stairwell and my bedroom door—the Cross of Saint Benedict. This potent emblem shields me; Camilla cannot ascend these stairs nor enter this

sanctuary. As long as I remain within, I am safe.

Camilla has entwined herself around you over countless nights, feeding on your essence until you became inseparable from her existence. Each drop binds you tighter; every sigh shared has become her breath of life. You are no mere lover—you are her lifeline among throngs who are just sustenance.

This dark bond bestows upon you a singular power—the power to end her eternity by claiming her black heart. Remember those nights you spent exploring each other's thresholds with blades dancing against skin? Turn that intimacy into your weapon; let seduction mask your intent until the fatal moment arrives.

Outside, Emiliano's desperation echoed through the hall as he pounded on the door. His own shouts pained him: "Elena, you ask too much! I cannot slay her—Camilla is beyond death!" Realizing his pleas vanished into silence, he retreated.

With a heavy heart, he wandered back towards his bedroom, the weight of his dilemma pressing him towards rest. He didn't know what to do next; perhaps a nap would help clear his head. Halfway along his path, an unsettling creak halted him—the sound of a door whispering secrets from shadows ahead. The corridor seemed to stretch infinitely as he approached cautiously, peering into its pitch-black void with mounting trepidation.

He leaned closer, heart pounding louder than before—afraid not of what lay beyond but of what it signified for his tormented existence caught between two women—one who was life itself...another who was life's antithesis.

Heart pounding, he tried to peer inside but was met with pitch-black darkness. Nothing was visible, only the unsettling chill emanating from within. Stepping closer tentatively, he squinted into the void once more.

Suddenly, something grabbed him by the shirt and yanked him inside with an unyielding force. He struggled against the iron grip that lifted him off the ground before throwing him backwards onto something soft like a large bed, as comfortable as his own yet unfamiliar.

"Who the fuck are you? What do you want? I'll kill you!" he screamed into the darkness.

A small ball of white light flickered into existence before him, growing larger and brighter until it illuminated Elena standing at the foot of the bed. She wore a loose-fitting white dress reminiscent of what he'd seen earlier in the garden, but now she slowly slipped it off her shoulders, letting it pool gracefully at her feet.

For the first time, Emiliano had an unobstructed view of Elena up close—absolute perfection incarnate. Her curvy silhouette was adorned with porcelain skin that seemed almost ethereal under the glow of light surrounding her. Full pouty lips parted slightly as she stared at him with piercing blue eyes that held secrets he desperately wanted to uncover.

Desire coursed through him. He couldn't tear his gaze away from her erect nipples—taut and inviting under the dim light. He wanted them with everything he had. But unlike others before him, he didn't seek possession; he yearned to worship them with his hands and lips.

Elena crawled onto the bed like a predatory feline, her movements slow and deliberate as she scaled his legs. With a practiced flick of her wrist, she stripped Emiliano of his clothes, ripping fabric in her haste. "What do I want, my love? I want to fuck you like you've never been fucked before," she whispered, her voice dripping with sin. "I want to remind you what you could have if you got rid of Camilla. I want your cock!"

Her words were gasoline on an already raging fire; just the sight of Elena had him hard. She stared hungrily at his length, a mix of awe and desire in her eyes as she wrapped both hands around it. She needed both hands to fully encompass it but yearned for its taste.

Elena lowered her head and licked from his balls up along the shaft's underside like an artist painting on canvas. When she reached the tip, she circled it with her tongue slowly, savoring every ridge. Emiliano could only moan in helpless surrender as he watched her work him over. The way her tongue flickered against him sent electric shocks through his body.

She slid him into her mouth inch by agonizing inch until he was buried deep in her throat—an impossible feat for anyone human. What is she? The thought was fleeting; lost as sensations overwhelmed him.

Pulling back with deliberate slowness, she let her lips caress him clean before straddling his hips. She pressed his cock against his stomach as she teased him with the heat of her pussy sliding back and forth over it without granting entry. He grinned at her teasing prowess.

Out of nowhere came a sharp slap across his face, followed by another from her other hand. "That's how you like to fuck, isn't it?" she demanded before slapping him again before he could respond.

Lost in sensation Emiliano just laid there enjoying the sensation of her pussy rubbing against his cock when he realized she had bound his hands to the bedframe with silk ties. Her pace was torturous as she lowered herself onto him bit by bit until he was fully inside her warmth.

She began riding slowly at first but quickly escalated as her body adjusted around his large cock—each thrust taking them higher into ecstasy.

"I have so much more for you, my love," Elena whispered seductively as long black nails emerged from her petite porcelain fingers. Her gaze locked onto Emiliano's eyes; she began to claw slowly but deeply from his shoulders down to his stomach. His skin split open under her touch, rivulets of blood trickling from each wound.

"Feel me," she commanded before slapping him hard across the face. Bringing a stinging pain that heightened his senses. She rubbed the fresh blood over his torso, painting him in crimson strokes before sliding off his cock. Bending low, she licked up every drop of blood from his body with deliberate slowness, savoring each taste.

Her mouth found its way back to his cock, sucking it until it was entirely coated in his own blood. With a drop still lingering on her lip, she climbed onto Emiliano's chest, grinding her wet pussy against his wounds until they both were slick with blood.

When her pussy was nice and bloody, she impaled herself on his cock. Riding him harder now as blood soaked into the sheets beneath them, she leaned forward with a wicked smile and wrapped her hands around his throat. Her grip tightened gradually as she began to cum on his cock.

This was what Emiliano craved; this is what he fucking loved—raw pain interwoven with intense pleasure. He felt himself teetering on the edge until he could no longer hold back and exploded inside her just as darkness claimed him again.

Pain jolted him awake; another slap across his face brought him back to reality—Elena was still riding him, though her grip on his throat had loosened slightly. Feeling her pussy on his cock and seeing her atop him brought another surge of arousal too powerful to resist as he approached climax once again.

Elena tightened her grip just as he began to cum again.

The cycle repeated—another punch woke him up only to see Elena meticulously licking all traces of blood and cum from his softening cock. She squeezed out every last drop before letting it fall back onto his stomach like an offering.

Rising from the bed with an ethereal glow fading from her body, she cast one lingering look over her shoulder at Emiliano. "That's how we will fuck when we're alone," she declared softly but firmly. "Only when I know you are fully mine can you do anything you want with my body. Get rid of Camilla!"

"Elena! My Love! Wait!" Emiliano screamed desperately as he broke free from his restraints and stumbled toward the door in a daze of adrenaline and longing. He banged furiously on Elena's bedroom door but received no response—only silence greeted him now.

Defeated and weakened by blood loss yet burning with unfulfilled desire, he staggered back into his room, where exhaustion overtook him instantly in heavy slumber filled with dreams colored red by both love and torment.

"You wanted my screams,"
she taunted through a deep laughter that echoed
across darkness thick enough
to suffocate hope itself. "Now give me yours."

CHAPTER 12

The Three Drunks

After her deliciously sinful playtime with Emiliano and Soledad, Camilla's hunger for new experiences led her to another nearby village. She wanted to walk around and get a feel for the village, but being a stunningly captivating succubus made blending in impossible.

From the moment she stepped foot into the village, every eye was drawn to her like moths to flame. Men ogled with unrestrained desire; women cast envious glances while secretly yearning for just a taste of what she offered.

Camilla wandered through vendors and curious onlookers until she reached a bustling pub nestled at the heart of the village. It thrummed with chaotic energy—a perfect hunting ground. She slipped into a dim corner at the back, ordering a dark red wine that matched her intentions for the evening.

Her piercing gaze caught three men eyeing her with drunken lechery from a darkened corner. Camilla's lips curled into a knowing smirk as she felt their intentions clawing at her back like desperate hands. They were amateurs at this game, their intent clear as crystal—a hunt they believed would end in their favor.

Pathetic fools, she mused silently. They sucked at following someone discreetly; their drunken swagger and loud whispers might as well have been neon signs announcing their pursuit.

She hadn't planned on indulging tonight—it was supposed to be just another reconnaissance—but fate always had a deliciously twisted sense of humor. And who was she to deny herself an easy meal?

Camilla made sure they noticed her nervous glances as she exited the pub. She selected an isolated alleyway, its darkness concealing all but those brave enough—or foolish enough—to follow.

The men's footsteps echoed behind her as she quickened her pace. With a calculated scream, she darted for the dark corner but stumbled intentionally.

Crumpled on the ground, she cried out, "Please! Don't hurt me! I just want to go home!" Her voice dripped with mock terror.

The men stood over her. "Don't worry your pretty head off," one sneered. "We'll take real good care of you."

They dragged her behind an ancient oak tree, where darkness consumed them. "No one will hear you scream here," growled the biggest of them. So, make those screams count. It will just make my dick harder.

Camilla shielded her face with her hands, hiding an amused smile as glints of sharp fangs peeked through her lips. "No... please stop! I've never even kissed a boy," she whimpered convincingly.

Brutally, they tore away her clothes while one slapped her hard across the face. "Shut up or this gets worse!" he snarled.

She muffled fake sobs as they exposed themselves. Camilla couldn't help but peek at their pathetic erections, stifling laughter behind trembling hands.

"One of you shut that bitch up!" barked the leader.

Camilla's heart raced as she felt the cold, unforgiving fingers entangle in her hair, yanking her head back with a brutal force. Her mouth was forced open as he thrust his cock between her lips, pushing deep into her throat. She made a show of gagging, the wet sounds echoing in the dimly lit alleyway—each one earning proud smirks from his onlooking friends.

"She can't handle this fat cock!" boasted the man in her mouth.

She felt another man grip her hips roughly, pulling her back onto his cock as he entered her pussy with a punishing rhythm. He rammed into her as if trying to break her spirit, falsely confident in his perceived dominance over her body. The third man didn't wait his turn; no, he invaded her ass without patience or finesse, groaning as he sank deeper inside.

They exchanged looks of triumph over her writhing form, their hands slapping each other's backs like gladiators sharing a victory. To them, Camilla was nothing more than a vessel for their conquest—a notion that amused her more than it horrified.

Camilla let out exaggerated moans and whimpers that echoed through the air, each cry meticulously calculated to feed their egos. Behind those tortured sounds was a mind calculating every move, every reaction.

Her eyes fluttered momentarily as she took control of the chaos within herself. Each thrust became an opportunity to reclaim her power in this twisted game of dominance and submission.

"Harder," she whispered around the cock in her mouth, her voice muffled yet clear enough to spur them on. "Make me feel it."

The words were bait—they always fell for it.

The men responded with renewed vigor as if they were truly conquering something valuable. Their breaths grew heavier, their movements more erratic as they pushed towards their own release.

Camilla inwardly smiled—a devious curve of satisfaction—as she pulled each string in this intricate play of power.

Growing bored with their antics, Camilla decided it was time for dessert. She bit down savagely on his cock and sucked his soul through the open wound. His moans of ecstasy turned into gasps of horror as his life drained away.

To his buddies, he is having a great time. "Make that bitch swallow it all!" his friends cheered. But he looks up and sees his body withering before them. All of a sudden, the empty skin bag falls to the floor. Both of the men scream in shock.

In their panic, they tried retreating only to find themselves trapped within Camilla's vise-like grip on their dwindling erections.

"Help! Please help me!" mocked Camilla with a dark laugh as she transitioned into her demon form, ready for a feast beyond flesh.

"You wanted my screams," she taunted through a deep laughter that echoed across darkness thick enough to suffocate hope itself. "Now give me yours."

Her wings expanded in an instant, lifting the three of them high above the village. The two men hung helplessly by their cocks; terror etched into their faces as they flew into an isolated dark area before being dropped onto the cold ground.

They screamed from both pain and fright as they hit the forest floor. Desperately searching around, they could only hear the ominous flapping of wings above.

One screamed as sharp talons raked across his back, yet nothing was visible in the darkness. The other tried to rise but collapsed when something sliced his Achilles tendon.

"What do you want with us? Please leave us alone!" one of them cried out in desperation.

A low, deep laugh resonated through the night air. "You forget you all followed me," Camilla's voice taunted from unseen angles.

"I remember you saying you'd take real good care of me. How was sticking those puny little worms you call cocks taking care of me? And you," she pointed at another man who visibly shuddered under her gaze, "you said hearing me cry for help made it hard. Funny how things turn soft when faced with real terror."

Camilla spat a ball of fire onto some dry wood on the ground, igniting an enormous blaze that illuminated her full demonic form—towering at seven feet tall with an expansive wingspan that cast ominous shadows over them.

"Are you here for our souls? Are you the devil himself?" one man cries out, his voice trembling with dread.

Camilla tilts her head back and laughs—a sound that chills the air around them. "Oh, sweetie," she purrs, "you're half right. I am here for your souls, but also for a little fun." Her eyes sparkle with malevolent delight. "The devil? Please! He's just an accountant these days—sign here, promise there. He's lost his taste for the game."

She steps closer, her wings unfurling majestically behind her, casting ominous shadows on the walls. "But I... I savor every drop of your fear," she whispered, her voice like silk over steel. "I relish your pain and bask in your anguish as life drains from your pathetic bodies."

This is fun for me; you should have let me leave quietly from that wretched pub," she chided softly. "Now it's my turn to play." Camilla's laugh echoed around them again as she added, "Cry for help all you want; beg for mercy if you must—it makes my tail fucking hard!" A wicked smile spread across her face.

With a swift movement, she seized the nearest man like he weighed nothing more than a feathered toy. Her wings lifted him effortlessly into the air as her talons sank into his flesh with ruthless precision.

His scream was a symphony to her ears.

Under her swirling skirts of darkness, her tail morphed into a thick cock adorned with scaled ridges that promised both agony and ecstasy.

"You enjoyed it rough when it was my pussy," she taunts before ramming her tail-cock into his ass. His scream echoes in the night as she pierces him mercilessly. "That's it, baby, take it all!" She drives deeper until he's impaled completely. "Fuck you were so tight, baby!"

She laughs as she pulls his lifeless body into her demon pussy, swallowing him whole in one smooth motion. She pauses momentarily to revel in the sensation of fucking herself with his corpse still inside her. That's how mommy likes it! She moans.

Camilla turned slowly, her gaze locking onto the other man, who was now screaming at the top of his lungs. A sinister smile curled on her lips. "I wasn't going to forget about you, baby," she whispered into his ear, her breath hot and tantalizing against his skin. "I have a new position for you; I've been thinking about this one for a while. I hope you love it as much as I do."

With an iron grip on his head, she caressed his cheek gently with one hand while her other transformed—a talon sharp enough to slice through bone in one swift motion. His head dropped to the ground with a dull thud. Laying back with an almost content sigh, she picked up the skull and admired it before using it as a fleshlight as she fucked it with her tail-cock.

Her wings morphed seamlessly into thick cocks—one invading the man's ass while another plunged into the gaping neck wound where his head once sat. Camilla moaned deeply, lost in pleasure as she fucked his lifeless body with predatory fervor.

"Fuuuuuck!" Her voice echoed through the night as she climaxed, dark cum oozing out from every orifice of his mutilated form. With an unholy hunger in her eyes, she opens her mouth wide and swallows the skull whole, savoring every drop of herself within it.

Licking her lips clean of remnants, she glanced at the fire she'd prepared earlier—a beacon of desolation amidst the night's tranquility. Her wings hoisted what remained of him over the flames as she watched intently, waiting until the flesh charred just right.

Laying back under the vast canopy of stars, she tore into his crisped remains with fervor while murmuring to herself between bites, "A good fuck always makes me hungry."

Once satiated, she rubbed her full belly with satisfaction and laughed uncontrollably into the darkness around her. "These fucking idiots! Do they think I'm the devil? Baby Lucifer wishes he was me! I do sadistic shit even he can't fathom." Am I the devil? Fucking morons.

As exhaustion from her macabre pleasures took over, Camilla closed her eyes against nature's silent backdrop. Tomorrow would bring new stories to share with her love Emiliano.

"Love is pain," he muttered under his breath,
recalling her own words
that had once been whispered in their
most intimate moments.
"Let's see how well you understand pain now,
my goddess."

CHAPTER 13

Elena Unmasked

Camilla landed gracefully at the hacienda, her senses immediately honing in on Emiliano—slumped on a garden bench like a broken statue. She slid beside him, her fingers tracing invisible patterns on his arm before enveloping him in an embrace. "Tell me what haunts you so deeply, my love?" she whispered, her lips grazing his ear with every word. "Whatever it is, we'll conquer it together."

Emiliano lifted his gaze, eyes shimmering with unshed tears. "Camilla, mi amor," he began, voice trembling yet resolute. You are my universe. It's always been us against the world. But I have failed you, my love. There is another woman here at the villa. She is blonde and beautiful, with porcelain-white skin. She only comes to me in my dreams, and we fuck.

She lives behind the large door at the end of the hall with the large cross on it. And those same crosses are on the stairs leading up to it. She says you cannot cross those; she is protected behind those symbols. But that is not the worst of it. She wants me to kill you. She wants me to destroy you so that she and I can be together forever. But I could never do that to you, my love. I could never break our union! Please believe me, my love! I am yours forever. Siempre y para siempre, mi amor!" Emiliano pleaded.

Camilla stood up slowly and walked away from Emiliano. He began to speak, but she just pointed a finger at him to not say a word. After several steps, she dropped to her knees and buried her face in her hands. Emiliano thought he heard her crying. He had never heard Camilla show any emotion before. What had he done? How could he ruin everything they had together? He got up and walked up behind her, placing his hand on her shoulder. She softly placed her hand over his.

Her cries began to get louder and louder until they were thunderous laughter. "Destroy me? Protected by those pathetic symbols? Her voice climbed an octave higher into maniacal delight. She quickly got up and turned around to face Emiliano.

"After all this time, do you not recognize who commands your soul?" Camilla's words cut through the air as she circled him like a predator savoring its prey.

"I know all about your blonde whore in this hacienda." Camilla's laughter echoed through the room, a sinister melody that sent shivers down Emiliano's spine. "I let that little bitch have her fun with you so you wouldn't get bored while I was out. I knew you couldn't leave, so why not leave you a plaything?"

I sensed that little whore the moment we pulled up." Camilla said, still laughing. Emiliano's eyes searched hers for any sign of anger. "So, you're not upset at me, my love?"

Never, my love." Her voice dripped with dark affection as she caressed his cheek. "Our union cannot be broken—not by that little lying bitch!"

Sitting beside him, she leaned closer, whispering. Has she even told you what she really is? Her true name?"

"No," Emiliano replied, curiosity piqued. "I thought maybe she was a ghost."

"She wishes," Camilla sneered. "She's no human or ghost. Not even a demon. She's an Egyptian goddess—Ammit the Devourer! Cast out when no one needed her judgment anymore. She used to sit on her throne and judge the dead to see if they would be allowed in their version of Heaven or Hell." "She is very judgmental! Well, when that no longer was needed, she was cast out."

Her grip tightened on his hand. "Now she roams as a goddess of retribution, consuming souls of sinners, and you're atop her list."

A goddess? Emiliano's interest darkened with intrigue.

"Yes," she nodded slowly, savoring his reaction. "She wants me gone so she can claim your soul." She has some of the similar powers that I have. She can shapeshift, she can glamor, and she can fly. But her powers are nowhere near mine.

"What shall we do with her?" Emiliano's lips curled into a wicked grin as his eyes lingered over her struggling form.

"Leave her to me," he replied confidently, his voice dripping with malicious intent. "You shattered the glamour spell; now she's at our mercy. I can already envision all the depraved acts I'll inflict upon this so-called goddess bitch."

With a predatory gleam in his eyes, Emiliano pulled her close. Their lips clashed in a fervent kiss, a mingling of shared cruelty and raw desire that sent shivers down both their spines. His hand gripped her hair tightly, asserting his dominance as she yielded reluctantly.

"Our love is unique, mi amor," Emiliano whispered against her lips, his words laced with both devotion and menace. "We embrace each other's darkness, don't we? You know every vile act I've committed just as I know yours. And yet, our love remains pure—twisted but pure. And with all of that we love each other completely. I would rip my still beating heart from my chest and hand it to you, if that is what you asked of me, my love." He pressed another deep kiss on her lips, filled with desperate passion.

He moved away reluctantly, his eyes still locked on hers, before turning towards the firewood area behind the hacienda. He picked up the heaviest ax available and meticulously began sharpening its blade on a nearby grinder.

"Love is pain," he muttered under his breath, recalling her own words that had once been whispered in their most intimate moments. "Let's see how well you understand pain now, my goddess."

Satisfied with the ax's sharpness after testing it on some wood, he walked back to the front of the hacienda and kicked open the door with a force that shook its foundations. Standing amidst the splintered wood, he called out into the void, "Elena, my love! I have great news for you! Elena, where are you?" His voice echoed through empty hallways as he began his ascent up the grand staircase.

Each step creaked under his weight as he dragged the heavy ax behind him; its metallic scrape against the tiles was a sinister symphony of impending doom. "I've made my decision, my love!" he declared loudly, each word dripping with manic conviction, reverberating off the cold stone walls.

He moved toward the large wooden door adorned with an ornate Saint Benedict Cross that seemed almost mocking in its sanctity. His fingers trailed over its gold lines tenderly at first as memories flooded back—Elena's laughter echoing in this very hallway, her scent lingering like a ghost. He whispered against it, "Open the door, my love. Let me tell you my decision: a future where nothing else matters but us."

He paused for a moment; desperation tinged his voice as he continued, "I've thought about what you mean to me... how unbearable it would be to lose your love." He imagined her on the other side, beautiful, fragile—and it both shattered and enraged him.

The smile left his face abruptly; anger surged in its place as darkness clouded his eyes. Leaning the ax against the doorframe with deliberate carelessness, he began pounding on it first with one fist, then both intensity growing with each blow. "Open this fucking door, you bitch!" he roared, fury turning his love-laced words into venomous spits.

With each strike against thick wood denting under assault and fragments of gold flying off like broken promises, the contrast between sweet longing and brutal aggression amplified every ounce of tension within those walls.

"My love, forgive me for overreacting." Emiliano's voice trembled with a mix of genuine sorrow and unhinged fury. "I don't mean any harm... I just want to fucking gut you, whore!" His eyes blazed as he picked up the ax, its cold weight familiar in his grip.

"Elena," he spat her name like a curse, "that's right... Not Ammit, the goddess whore!" He brought the blade closer to his face, licking its sharp edge slowly until blood welled up on his tongue. The metallic taste mingled with his rage, pushing him further towards madness.

He spat crimson droplets onto the ax blade before letting them splatter onto the door. "Honey, I'm fucking home!" he roared, swinging the ax with relentless fury. Each strike echoed through the house like a death knell.

Outside in the garden, Camilla's lips curled into a satisfied smile. She knew Emiliano was handling matters as only he could. She leaned back against a stone bench, her eyes half-closed in pleasure at the sounds emanating from inside—the rhythmic thud of wood being cleaved apart.

Every swing took a toll on the thick, dense door separating him from his prize. Emiliano's muscles strained under the effort; sweat mingled with blood as it dripped off his chin. His size and strength were formidable in any situation, but fueled by rage and lust for dominance, nothing could stand against him for long.

As each splinter flew from the doorframe, memories surged within him—nights spent tracing Elena's skin under moonlight now tainted by betrayal. The anticipation built with every blow; soon enough, nothing would be left to hold him back from claiming what was his.

After what felt like an eternity of relentless assault, Emiliano finally breached the barrier, the splintering wood giving way under his unwavering determination. Darkness loomed beyond the jagged hole he'd created, its ominous void calling him forward. Each violent swing chipped away at the door with renewed fervor until it succumbed entirely to his forceful kicks, slamming open against the wall with a deafening crash.

"You're fucked now, bitch!" Camilla's voice floated in from outside, laced with malevolent satisfaction.

Emiliano's familiarity with the room's layout was his advantage now. He knew where each shadow lay hidden. He flung his axe towards the shrouded windows, its blade slicing through heavy drapes that had kept daylight at bay. Sunlight poured into the room, banishing shadows as Emiliano's gaze fixed upon the motionless figure on the bed.

Elena lay there, her blonde hair stark against her white veil, like an angel trapped in a nightmare. Her body was wrapped in that infamous thin white dress—a haunting vision of purity corrupted by darkness.

"Oh my love," Emiliano sneered as he advanced towards her prone form. "Our time together has just begun. No need to play dead for my sake—you'll get there soon enough."

His hand encircled her throat effortlessly, lifting her as though she weighed nothing at all. There was something disturbingly light about her—the kind of lightness born from death itself. "You'll regret crossing us, Elena... Ammit... whatever your fucking name is!" he roared as he tore away her veil.

What met his eyes froze him in place—what the fuck is this—a fusion of beauty turned grotesque? Shiny golden hair lay against a decayed, shriveled face from which pieces of flesh fell away like dust from ancient parchment.

Ripping off her white dress revealed more of this macabre sight—her entire body shared the same ghastly transformation as her face. Patches of grayish skin were missing; sections looked eerily familiar.

"It can't be!" he whispered hoarsely as recognition dawned upon him. He seized one of Elena's letters from the bedside table and held it against her corpse—the discolored paper fit perfectly into her missing skin patches.

"The fucking paper was her skin! Vintage indeed," he muttered incredulously before noticing something even more sinister: Her right index finger sharpened into a bony point-stained crimson—a grotesque pen dipped in blood ink for writing those cursed letters.

His rage ignited anew; he broke apart her skull effortlessly and flung it against a wall, where it shattered into countless fragments before smashing what remained of her skeleton onto the bed until only dust remained.

"Face me!" he bellowed into emptiness. Enough games! I won't leave until you've drawn your last breath."

A sudden burst of light radiated above the bed—blinding yet alluring as it merged into Elena's form once more but transformed beyond recognition. Her porcelain skin now roughened like chalk; jet-black lips contrasting sharply against pale flesh; soulless black eyes reflecting untold depths of darkness; long black nails extending from skeletal fingers as she descended gracefully onto solid ground yet hovered ethereally.

Her voice thundered through him like divine judgment: "You insignificant man... I am Ammit—the Devourer—and today I claim your soul for all your heinous deeds!"

"You are going to die, bi." Emilano's voice faltered as her predatory gaze locked onto him, silencing him with sheer intensity.

Elena's hand wrapped around his throat with an iron grip, her nails digging into his skin like deadly talons. His arrogant smirk disappeared, replaced by a flicker of fear.

"Stupid little man," she hissed, her voice a sultry mix of venom and allure that echoed through the dimly lit room. The air around them grew thick with an otherworldly energy as she continued, "I am Ammit, the Devourer."

Her eyes burned with a divine fury, reflecting centuries of wrathful judgment. "For every vile act you've committed," her voice lowered to a dangerous whisper that sent shivers down his spine, "your time has come."

Emiliano's eyes widened as her grip tightened. He tried to speak, but only a strangled gasp escaped him. "Elena..." he managed to choke out.

A cruel smile curled her lips as she leaned closer, her breath hot against his ear. "No more words, my love," she purred before plunging her clawed hand into his chest with a sickening crunch.

He could feel each excruciating second of pain as her fingers wrapped around his heart, pulling it free from its cavity with agonizing slowness. She held it before his fading vision, blood dripping from her hand like a grisly trophy.

As darkness claimed him, he heard her final words echoing in his mind—a twisted lullaby laced with triumph and finality.

"Your story ends here." —his body collapsing onto cold floorboards beneath them both as she relished displaying his life essence.

Elena stood over Emiliano's lifeless body, her fingers curling around his still-warm heart. "I'm sorry it had to end this way, my love," she murmured, a seductive lilt in her voice. "The sex was incredible. But your soul is mine." She laughed softly as she raised the heart to her lips, ready to consume it.

As she prepared to swallow it whole, it pulsed one last time before crumbling into dust and slipping through her grasp like sand through fingers. Panic flickered in her eyes as she hissed in frustration, "This can't be! I will have to take his soul the old way!"

Determined, Elena lifted Emiliano's cold body from the ground and pressed her lips to his in a kiss meant to claim his essence—an intimate act that had claimed many before him. She kissed him again, deeper each time, but felt no transfer of energy, not even a spark.

Suddenly, Emiliano's eyes snapped open, their depths now an endless black void staring back at her. A wicked grin spread across his face as he growled, "Are we going to fuck or not? I crave more than your kiss, Elena. I want my cock in that little wet pussy of yours." His hand moved swiftly to grasp her throat with unanticipated strength.

Stunned by his defiance and strength despite having no heart, Elena struggled against his iron grip. Her mind raced: how could a mere human withstand death's kiss? And why did he seem stronger than ever?

"You really thought you could rid yourself of me so easily?" Emiliano's voice dripped with venomous amusement as he tightened his hold on her throat.

Elena began to glow with an ethereal light that grew brighter with each passing second until it exploded outward in a brilliant flash. The force flung Emiliano across the room and out through a window.

Landing hard on the gravel outside, he scrambled to his feet only to find Elena had encased the hacienda in a shimmering sphere of light, a barrier he couldn't breach no matter how much he pounded against it.

Glancing down at his chest, where there should have been an open wound, he instead found smooth, unmarked skin where his heart had once been torn out. "How the fuck am I alive? His voice echoed with confusion laced heavily with anger as he surveyed the vicinity for any sign of Camilla who might aid him, saying aloud, "Where's the fuck is Camilla? A little help would have been nice."

"I felt the darkness in your heart and soul.
I sensed what you
could become—unlike the others."
She paused, letting her hand drift down his chest
teasingly before gripping him firmly
through his trousers.
"And that cock... It was made for me alone!"

CHAPTER 14

Emiliano

Emiliano circled the glowing orb until he reached the garden in the back. Camilla lounged on a stone bench, her eyes following him like a predator stalking prey.

"Where were you? I needed your help! I could have died back there!" Emiliano's voice trembled with lingering fear and frustration.

A slow smile curled on Camilla's lips. "Did you die? She chuckled, low and menacing.

"Yeah, what the fuck was that about? Why am I not dead? Where is my heart?" His voice escalated into a scream.

Camilla stood in one fluid motion, her eyes gleaming with cold amusement. before she slapped him hard enough to send him sprawling onto the grass. "Quit your whining, little baby! You can't die—not easily anyway."

She stood over him as he lay stunned. "Did you really think I'd fall in love with a mere mortal? A fucking human! You're something far more extraordinary, you're a Cambion! One of the most evil, sadistic—and, not to mention, one of the fucking hottest creatures I've ever encountered."

"What's a Cambion? What am I?" Emiliano's voice was barely above a whisper now.

"Sit down," she commanded as she guided him back to the bench. "You're no longer human." "You're part human, part demon—your soul was human until Ammit ripped out your heart. In that moment, you transformed into your superior form—a full Incubus. I know you have questions, so ask them?"

"How am I a Cambion?" he asked shakily.

Camilla's eyes softened briefly as she delved into memories both bitter and sweet. "Remember how I saved you from your father and those vile men?

Her breath hitched, eyes flashing with a mix of fury and vulnerability.

"Your father was an Incubus, a formidable demon. Those men—demons too—thought you'd follow in their footsteps. But when you were born a Cambion, they mistook you for nothing more than human." He stepped closer, his presence overwhelming, her words dripping with unspoken promises.

"They raped your mother repeatedly." Her tone grew colder, sharper. "When she failed to birth another Incubus, they took her soul as punishment. And then they set their sights on you, waiting for puberty to reveal your true nature."

The memories flooded back—dark nights filled with torment he could never escape. "When you didn't change," she continued, eyes locking onto his with predatory intensity, "they despised you even more. But I could sense the difference in you from miles away."

She traced a finger along his jawline, eliciting a shiver that traveled down his spine. "That night in the barn," she murmured, "When I saw their hands on you... I couldn't stand by." Her grip tightened ever so slightly. "Incubi are powerful demons with many abilities. But they're no match for me—not at my level."

She leaned in closer, her breath hot against his ear. "You owe me everything," she whispered, the threat mingling with desire in her voice. "And I intend to collect."

"That night, under the blood-red moon, I glamoured you. I poured venomous hate and seething anger into your mind." My evil coursed through your veins, guiding you to do what needed to be done. Any demon that dared get close, I took care of them."

Emiliano's eyes flickered as he recalled it all—the exhilarating surge of power with each kill, blood-curdling screams igniting a dark hunger within him. But confusion clouded his memories as well. "Why me, Camilla? Why did you choose a half-breed used as a plaything by demons? What did you see in me?"

"My love," Camilla purred, stepping closer so her breath warmed his neck. "I felt the darkness in your heart and soul. I sensed what you could become—unlike the others." She paused, letting her hand drift down his chest teasingly before gripping him firmly through his trousers. "And that cock... It was made for me alone! But don't think it was love at first sight."

A wicked smile danced on her lips as she continued, "I devour souls and male cum to regenerate my strength. Every time I consumed yours... we became connected in ways unbreakable even by death itself." Her nails dug into his skin possessively. "Our love—born from hellfire's light—is unyielding!"

Emiliano's breath hitched under her touch, but questions still lingered unanswered within him. "So now I'm an Incubus? What does that mean for me?"

There are wonderful things awaiting you," Camilla promised with a dark gleam in her eye as she outlined his new abilities: shapeshifting into anything desired; glamouring humans effortlessly; controlling lesser demons minds; possessing immense strength beyond any mortal's reach; manipulating energy; teleportation;

telekinesis—all requiring practice but achievable nonetheless.

Watching him attempt to shoot fire from his hands only producing sparks earned a laugh from Camilla, a mix of endearment wrapped in exasperation—"Fuck me! Sometimes this age gap really shows! Stop playing around." She tilted his chin towards him harshly yet affectionately before turning serious again. "We have unfinished business—we need to take care of this stupid bitch!"

"Yes!" Emiliano replied fiercely as new determination kindled within those now-blackened eyes while walking toward Elena's radiant barrier, ready for confrontation—a real demon born anew under Camilla's shadowy tutelage.

"As her soul fully entered Emiliano,
a surge of energy and power flooded through him.
With a deep guttural moan,
he climaxed inside the fleshy vessel
that was left behind."

CHAPTER 15

The Incubus

Emiliano reached out into the glowing light, feeling its energy course through his veins like molten fire. His eyes fluttered shut as he absorbed its potent force, remembering the whispered promises of power that Camilla had instilled in him. With each heartbeat, his body consumed more of the brilliant glow until it began to wane around the hacienda, leaving him shrouded in an eerie black glow.

"Where are you, Ammit?" His voice rolled out like thunder, low and menacing. Shadows danced in response as he commanded the doors open with newfound telekinesis, striding purposefully up the creaking stairs. "Enough fucking games! Face me!"

From within the gathering dusk of Elena's room, light began to pulse once again. Elena emerged from behind a wall, levitating serenely yet imposingly above the ground, her black-clawed finger pointing directly at him.

"So you were never human," she hissed, her voice dripping with scornful pleasure. "Camilla, that bitch hid your secret well. But as a demon, you're just an infant." A blinding blast of white energy erupted from her hand, slamming Emiliano against the wall with brutal force.

Pinned by her radiant power, he felt every nerve in his body crackle in defiance as Elena's laughter echoed around him, a haunting melody that sent shivers down his spine. Her eyes glowed with an unholy light, locking onto his with a predatory gaze that promised both pleasure and pain.

"You're no match for me," she purred, each word dripping with a lethal mix of seduction and scorn. "You are but an infant—naive enough to think you could destroy me."

She stepped closer, her presence overwhelming him like a suffocating wave of heat. The scent of her perfume—a dark, intoxicating blend of roses and sin—invaded his senses.

"And as for that whore, she won't save you," she taunted, her voice lowering to a dangerous whisper that danced along his skin like a caress.

He gritted his teeth harder, blood rushing through his veins like liquid fire as he struggled against her hold. His mind was a chaotic storm of defiance and desire; he despised her dominance yet craved the touch that sent electric jolts through his body.

"Elena..." he growled her name through clenched teeth, each syllable laced with both hatred and longing.

She smiled at his futile resistance, a cruel twist of her lips that promised a pleasure he'd never forget—and a torment he'd never escape.

"Let's see how long you can resist," she murmured, leaning in so close that her breath mingled with his—a whisper of warmth against his lips before she claimed them in a searing kiss that shattered whatever resolve he had left.

But Emiliano recalled Camilla's teachings—the latent abilities that lay dormant within him waiting to be unleashed. His eyes ignited with an obsidian glow as he focused on Elena, lifting her effortlessly before slamming her against the ceiling.

The impact broke her concentration; she released him as he wrestled control back with ferocity fueled by rage and pain. He hurled her across the room like a rag doll until she collided brutally with an iron bed frame post he had manipulated into a deadly spike.

Elena's light dimmed as blood splattered from her mouth; she hung lifelessly impaled upon the wrought iron. "I told you I would fucking end you," Emiliano spat out triumphantly as he turned away.

Suddenly laughter—cold and mocking—filled the air once again. He spun around to see Elena rise from death's grip unscathed, her luminescence now blindingly painful.

"You are really fucking stupid. You really thought it would be that easy?" She sneered before launching into rapid strikes that left him gasping and disoriented in her dazzling wake.

She moved with lightning speed, making it nearly impossible for Emiliano to track her movements. As she struck again and again, he was forced to fight blind, his vision consumed by the brightness of her attack. Despite swinging in every direction, he couldn't seem to land a hit, only feeling the sting of her razor sharp claws against his skin. But they both understood that these attacks were more of an annoyance, than a true danger to Emiliano.

This time though, Emiliano was ready; he closed his eyes against her brilliance and extended his arm instinctively, catching her by the throat mid-strike—a gamble that paid off gloriously as she struggled in vain against his crushing grip.

With brutal precision, he plunged his free hand into her chest; black light surged forth explosively until Elena shattered in incandescent fragments around him.

Exhausted yet victorious, Emiliano staggered down the hall toward his bedroom balcony, where Camilla awaited below a vision of patient dread interwoven with hope.

"It's done," he called down hoarsely yet victoriously, only for cold steel reality to stab through his spine; Elena's spectral hand ripped cruelly through him, glowing ominously once again from within.

"Hurts, doesn't it? You stupid fuck!" She whispered venomously, looking down at Camilla with malevolent glee burning brightly in each word uttered. "He's all yours now, demon bitch."

"I fucked him plenty already!" Elena screamed as the incandescent light swelled until an explosion tore through Emiliano's chest. She tossed his limp body off the balcony with a grace that belied her strength before flying off into the night sky, her silhouette disappearing against the moonlit horizon.

Camilla watched her leave, her eyes glowing with an inner fire that mirrored her burning rage. Slowly, she approached Emiliano's crumpled form on the ground. Kneeling beside him, she placed a trembling hand against his head, feeling his warmth seep back into his cooling skin.

"Amor... you do love me," Emiliano whispered as he opened his eyes to see Camilla hovering over him, tears glistening in her eyes like dew drops on a poisoned flower. "I knew you did. I'm sorry I failed you."

"Shut up!" Camilla snapped, though her voice betrayed a hint of weariness. "My eyes are watery because I had flames shooting out of them." She smirked slightly, trying to disguise her relief at seeing him alive. "You didn't fail me; we can still go after her. But seriously, when did you become such an emotional bitch? Cut it out already! You're a fucking demon now."

Emiliano sensed the authority in her words and swallowed hard. He felt a strange mix of fear and desire as she spoke, an intoxicating blend of emotions he couldn't quite decipher.

"She's heading for a village I've visited before," Camilla said thoughtfully, her mind already strategizing their next move. "I have an idea of what she's planning. But we need our strength first. I'll fetch us some souls."

Before Emiliano could respond, Camilla dissolved into an ominous black mist that swirled around him before vanishing into the night. Left alone with his thoughts, he turned toward their villa, determined not to fail again.

Closing his eyes, he focused on his bedroom, willing himself there through sheer force of will. When he opened them again, he found himself standing not in his room but in their pool, his pants soaking wet.

"Damn it," he muttered under his breath with a frustrated shake of his head. "I need more practice with this."

Determined to master his new abilities, Emiliano climbed out of the water and focused once more—this time feeling a searing desire for vengeance course through him like liquid fire.

Camilla emerged from the shadows; her gaze fixed on the flickering flames of a bonfire that illuminated an isolated clearing. The laughter and carefree chatter of eight individuals echoed through the night, oblivious to the lurking danger. A black mist materialized before them, drawing every eye as it morphed into a mesmerizingly beautiful woman.

Naked and smiling wickedly, Camilla stood before them, her mere presence casting an irresistible spell. With a mere glance, Camilla ensnared them entirely. The four women rose as if guided by an unseen force, their hands trembling as they shed their clothes while approaching her. Each step was a testament to their surrender. She watched their clothes fall away with a predatory satisfaction; these were offerings for Emiliano, a necessity for his eminent battle.

The women surrounded her, kissing and caressing her skin in reverent worship. A girl kneeled before her, pressing eager lips against Camilla's pussy. "That's it baby! Take care of mama!" she moaned, lost in the haze of pleasure as two others suckled at her breasts. The last traced delicate lines down her back before spreading Camilla's cheeks wide, tongue delving into forbidden territory.

Camilla's eyes glinted dangerously as she motioned to the first man. He shivered under her disappointed gaze but obeyed nonetheless, stripping bare before reluctantly approaching. She gripped his head tenderly yet firmly, locking lips in a lethal embrace that drained him completely before discarding his lifeless body.

Her attention returned to the women who worshipped her flesh without respite. "More," she whispered with dark hunger as she beckoned another man forward. He too failed to meet expectations but served his purpose as she drained him dry with her kiss of death.

Camilla's eyes glinted with an insatiable hunger as she watched the writhing bodies around her. She craved everything they had to offer but wouldn't ruin them, at least not yet.

One girl latched onto Camilla's serpentine tail, lips working feverishly as if her life depended on it, while Camilla fingered the other two. The girl beneath her mouth was an artist in pleasure; Camilla's thighs quivered at every skillful lick. Interrupting such devotion would be sacrilege.

With a silent command, her eyes beckoned a third male forward, his presence a poor substitute for her beloved Emiliano—but necessity dictated indulgence over preference tonight. His cock was hard but unremarkable as it entered her mouth; still, she enveloped him with expert precision.

Each pulse against her tongue reminded her cruelly of Emiliano's potent touch, absent yet omnipresent in every lover's failure to match him. As the man climaxed, Camilla gripped his hips with vice-like determination, milking every drop from him as though extracting his very essence.

The salty tang mingled on her tongue as his soul ebbed away through his release into her waiting mouth—a testament to her dominion over mortal desires.

When the last shudder left his now vacant body, she released him disdainfully, letting him crumple to the floor like discarded refuse. His lifeless form was nothing more than a fleeting diversion in her eternal quest for something or someone who could measure up to Emiliano.

Despite their shortcomings as lovers compared to Emiliano, they were necessary sustenance. She sucked eagerly on each remaining man until their souls were hers alone. "Enough!" she declared at last. "It's time. Come with me, ladies! I have a special surprise waiting for you!"

With supernatural grace, she gathered the women and flew towards Emiliano's stronghold under a moonlit sky. Landing softly before him, she let her prizes tumble at his feet like discarded dolls.

"There's my property!" she purred seductively as she freed Emiliano's throbbing cock from confinement. Every stroke of her mouth was both worshipful and possessive until Emiliano groaned with need. "Fuck, I missed this, my love!" She said as she took him deeper into her mouth.

Camilla moved with calculated grace, bringing each of the women over to Emiliano one by one. She positioned the first girl on her back, guiding Emiliano's eager cock into her waiting pussy. "Fuck her, my love!" Camilla whispered in his ear, urging him on. And fuck her he did, with a ferocity that made the girl moan loudly and clutch at the grass beneath her.

"Now kiss her, my love," Camilla instructed, as Emiliano continued his rhythm. "When your lips touch, picture the energy of her soul within her. Connect with that and suck it in your kiss." Emiliano focused intently on Camilla's words as he tentatively leaned down to press his lips against the dying girl's. He could feel her life force pulsating through him, and he held onto it tightly as he tried his first death kiss.

As their lips touched and their souls connected, Emiliano felt a rush of energy flow into him from the dying girl. Her body withered away even as she tightened around his cock, bringing him to a climax unlike any he had ever experienced before. He was consumed with both pleasure and a strange sense of power as he absorbed her soul into his own being.

As her soul fully entered Emiliano, a surge of energy and power flooded through him. With a deep guttural moan, he climaxed inside the fleshy vessel that was left behind. Camilla, always quick on her feet, ran over to him and began sucking him clean, eager to consume every last bit of energy she could get from his release. Then, with a swift movement, she moved to the dead body and sucked out all traces of Emiliano's cum, absorbing it into her own body to reinforce her strength.

This ritual continued with the other three girls who had joined them. One by one, Emiliano collected their souls, and Camilla consumed their essence, each time feeling more energized and powerful than ever before.

"The collecting of souls is far better than playing with nipples, mi amor!" Emiliano exclaimed as he looked down at himself in amazement. He spoke almost to himself, lost in the euphoria of his newfound strength and abilities. Meanwhile, Camilla remained focused on draining Emiliano completely of his cum, determined to strengthen herself as much as possible.

When she was satisfied, they both lay back under the dark night sky, breathing heavily from their exertions. "Rest now, my love," Camilla whispered lovingly to

Emiliano. "Soon we will finish off that bitch once and for all." She leaned in to give him a passionate kiss before they both closed their eyes and drifted off into a deep slumber, ready to face whatever challenges might come their way in the morning.

"Oh, poor naive Camilla," Ammit sighed mockingly.
"There is power in this church.
During the Spanish Inquisition, this very ground
was saturated with its own brand of darkness
in an attempt to combat earthly evils."

CHAPTER 16

Ammit's Plan

Elena approached a village nestled in the midst of rolling green hills and fields. The quaint houses and buildings were surrounded by lush gardens and colorful flowers, creating a picturesque scene. However, there was something about this particular village that drew Elena to it. As she neared the center of the town, her eyes were immediately drawn to an old church perched at the top of a hill.

The church's ancient stone walls and towering steeple gave off an eerie aura, as if it held secrets from centuries past. It was said to have been in service during the Spanish Inquisition, a time when unspeakable acts were committed in the name of God. But despite its dark history, Elena could sense a lingering power, within its walls—the power of prayer and evil, intertwined in a battle for dominance.

With determined steps, Elena ascended the stone steps leading up to the church.

The intricate craftsmanship of its design became more apparent as she stepped through its doors. The high vaulted ceilings with stunning stained-glass windows depicted scenes of bloodshed and torture from the inquisition. Yet, there was a certain beauty in the way the colors danced across the stone floors.

As she made her way down the aisle towards the stage, she could feel the presence of dark forces surrounding her. Placing her hand on the large wooden cross at the front, Elena chanted powerful words: "With all the power granted to me as Ammit, the Devourer, I claim this house as my own." She could feel the energy building within her as she claimed ownership over this place and its people.

Suddenly, priests emerged from a back room and dropped to their knees before Elena's glowing figure. They had never seen anyone like her before—with blonde hair cascading down her porcelain skin and black eyes, lips, and nails adorning her body. Dressed in a thin white gown that hugged her curves, she was a striking and formidable presence.

But the priests were not afraid. They immediately recognized her as Ammit and bowed their heads in reverence. Elena walked over to them, speaking in a calm yet commanding voice: "Do not fear, my children. I am here to save you, to protect you from evil. Join me in my fight against darkness. Pray to me, Ammit the Devourer."

As she waved her hand over them, the priests' eyes turned solid black, showing their devotion to Elena and her cause. With a nod of approval, she turned her attention back to the church and its congregation. One by one, she entered each home within the village, quickly baptizing each member into her growing army of followers.

With each person she converted, Elena could feel her power growing stronger. She reveled in her true form as Ammit, no longer hiding behind a human facade but embracing her identity as a powerful force of evil. As the night progressed, her army grew in size until it encompassed every single person in the village.

With an army at her command, Elena set out to spread her influence throughout the world—to banish every last trace of evil with her own brand of darkness. And as she walked through the streets of that small village, she knew that she had found a new home for herself and her disciples—a place where they would thrive and reign supreme as rulers of all that is wicked and twisted.

Camilla's wings flapped powerfully as she took off into the night, her destination set for a small village to the north. It was said that an old church stood there, steeped in history and secrets. Her eyes glimmered with excitement as she thought of what surprises may await her. there. As she flew, she could see the lights of the city below, bustling with life and unaware of the darkness that lurked just beyond its borders.

Meanwhile, Emiliano prepared himself for the teleportation jump. He had never attempted such a long distance before, and he felt a surge of nervous energy coursing through him. With Camilla's words echoing in his mind, he closed his eyes and focused on picturing the location she described. When he opened them again, he found himself standing in the middle of an open field, far from any sign of civilization. "Fuck, this is not right," he said angrily.

Frustrated, Emiliano closed his eyes once more and tried again. This time, he found himself in the same desolate spot. Determined not to give up, he closed his eyes one final time and focused all of his concentration on their destination. And when he opened his eyes again, he was just outside the city limits, gazing up at the old church perched atop a hill.

He didn't hear any screams of pain or fear, so he figured Camilla hadn't started yet. So he smiled and began walking into town.

Meanwhile, Camilla had already arrived at the church. She landed gracefully in the doorway and let out a laugh as she looked around at the peaceful surroundings. "You really think this place could harm me?" she taunted as she stepped inside.

The interior of the church was dimly lit by flickering candles near the cross at the front. "Quit hiding, Ammit!" Do you really think you can harm me? Camilla called out confidently, her exhaustion barely noticeable. But suddenly, a bright glow began to form near the candles as Ammit materialized before her.

"This is where you will take your last breath, demon!" Ammit declared with authority. "Your kind is not wanted here. I will banish you back to where you came from."

Camilla smirked, unfazed by the threat. But as she looked down, she noticed that she was standing on one of the Saint Benedict crosses etched into the floor. And surrounding her were a circle of priests, their eyes black as they chanted under their breath.

Camilla let out a low growl as she transformed into her full demon form, towering over them at seven feet tall with large black wings tinged with red. Her long black hair formed two massive horns that hung down past her shoulders. And her eyes glowed with a fiery red light, every inch the fearsome demon she truly was.

But even in this terrifying form, Camilla couldn't help but laugh at the priests and their futile attempts to stop her. "You honestly think this little piece of art and some praying men can defeat me?" She mocked, her forked snake tongue flicking between her sharp fangs. "They fear me in hell just as much as these weak humans fear me here." Camilla roars. Her full demon form is on display.

She tried to fly but found herself immobile. Panic surged as she attempted once more to move her legs and wings, only to remain stuck. "What have you done, you fucking bitch?" Camilla screamed, defiance lacing her voice despite the tremor of fear that rippled through her core.

"These are not normal priests, my dear Camilla," Ammit purred, her tone a dangerous mix of seduction and menace. "They are monks of Ammit. The combination of their prayer within my protection circle, along with my power to banish evil—it's what has you trapped. You can do nothing now but wait... and die! Her laughter echoed off the ancient walls.

"I'm sure you'd love to hear their special prayer, wouldn't you? Raise your voices, my children!" Ammit commanded with a sadistic glee.

The monks chanted in unison:

"Put on the entire armor of Goddess Ammit, that you may be able to stand against the schemes of evil, and the devil himself. May every demon, every evil spirit, and every cursed word against us be destroyed in the mighty name of Ammit. And may all evil be banished back to hell from whence it came!"

"Those are just words! How do they hold me against my will? How are you doing this?" Camilla demanded, shock and frustration intertwining in her voice.

"Oh, poor naive Camilla," Ammit sighed mockingly. "There is power in this church. During the Spanish Inquisition, this very ground was saturated with its own brand of darkness in an attempt to combat earthly evils. This curse lingers within these walls, amplifying my powers even without my followers."

The goddess's laughter grew uncontrollable as she continued, "This town, let me rebuild my congregation and magnify my strength through the wickedness stored here. You're being defeated by your own chaotic essence!"

Ammit motioned for a priest, who carefully handed her something wrapped in an old cloth. As she slowly unwrapped it, she smirked at Camilla's widening eyes. "You see, this church held a special gift for me—an ancient weapon capable of destroying you once and for all."

Her eyes gleamed as she revealed an ancient spearhead gleaming dully under flickering candlelight. "This is no ordinary weapon; it's the spear that pierced Jesus on the cross. Its divine power alone can send you back to hell for eternity." She savored each word as if tasting them on her tongue.

"I must prepare for your banishment," she whispered. Ammit dismissed herself to prepare for Camilla's banishment, leaving her enemy alone with her thoughts and fears. She urged Camilla to save her strength, for she would need it in the coming battle. And with that, Ammit vanished from sight, leaving Camilla to contemplate her fate at the hands of this powerful goddess and her devoted followers.

"You never learn, Emiliano.
But this time, I will not only kill you,
but I will also make your precious
Camilla watch as I rip off her tail
and use it to take her soul,"
she taunts as she flies towards him
with tremendous speed.

CHAPTER 17

I'll Burn This World For You

Emiliano stood at the entrance to the village. He was surprised that he hadn't seen any sign of Camilla or the fighting up to this point. If it wasn't that it was Camilla, he would be worried. He decided to continue to move forward. Stopping at the first buildings, he yells out, "I'm here for you, Ammit! Come out and face your death!"

That familiar glow appears before him. Ammit appears to be laughing at him uncontrollably. "You stupid little man. Your beautiful Camilla is already held prisoner in my church. And very soon we are going to kill her and send her back to hell!" "You fucking touch her, and I will burn this fucking village to the ground. I will see this entire world fucking burn before I let anything happen to her!" Emiliano says as a burst of black energy exits his hand and explodes at Ammit's feet. "Oh, I see you are starting to get a hang of it. Well, let me help you practice!" Ammit says as she disappears.

A large group of villagers who had become Ammit zombies, appear from behind the buildings. They walk towards Emiliano as he continues shooting the black energy bursts from his hands. There are too many approaching him for this to work as is. He notices some farm tools off to the side of the road.

Picking up the one with the largest blade on it, he rushes at the group. Swinging at every single one of them, trying to get through the crowd. But there are just too many of them to fight off alone. They grab Emiliano and try to carry him towards the church. "Camilla! I won't fucking let them hurt you, amor!" he yells. Just then he emits a bright black burst of energy from his body. It burns all that was holding him and knocks more off of their feet. He focuses and appears at the top of one of the buildings. Looking down, he sees that there are hundreds in Ammit's zombie army.

I need to come up with another plan, he thinks to himself. He tries to recall all the things that Camilla had told him about his powers. He remembered the part about his glamoring ability—that he also had the power to control demons. He had no idea what to do, but he was not going to let anything happen to Camilla. Even if that meant destroying this world in the process.

He began to glow in that bright black light again. It pulsed with the energy that was emitting from his body. He raised his arms high above his head and proclaimed the following: "All evil spirits that can hear my call, to all demons that this reaches. Rise and join me in our dark path of evil. Bring all those who hide in the shadows, those whose names are feared to be spoken. I summon you all to rise and join me to defeat the goddess Ammit!"

At first nothing happened, but soon the wind began to pick up. Black spirits appeared and flew through the crowd of Ammit's followers. Four large demons appeared behind the crowd as they started picking up the people and swallowing them whole. "These souls are for you! Feed to your black heart's desire!" Emiliano screams.

He jumps back down and begins swinging the blade to any person in front of him as he moves forward towards the church. Ammit's zombies were no match for Emiliano or the demons he summoned, as they were quickly being devoured from all sides. As the demons remove the last of the zombies, they turn and walk towards Emiliano. They stand in front of him waiting for their orders.

"Thank you, my demon brothers! I will go save our queen, Camilla. You may return to your home once more." Emiliano commands

Emiliano stands at the entrance of the church, his arms lifted to his sides as black spirits still swirl around him. With each passing moment, they merge with Emiliano's being, turning him into a vessel of pure evil. His eyes radiate a brilliant black hue, matching the dark aura emanating from his entire body. With a sudden burst of energy, he kicks open the doors and strides into the church with determination.

Inside, he finds his beloved Camilla in her demon form, chained above the cross on the floor. Rage consumes Emiliano as he charges towards her, yelling out her name. "You foolish bitch! I warned you that any harm to her would result in the destruction of this world!" He roars as he swiftly takes down each priest in his path, their necks breaking under his powerful grip.

With every chant silenced and every member of the prayer circle dead, Camilla is finally able to move again. As she struggles against her restraints, Emiliano focuses his dark energy onto the chains, causing them to explode and freeing her. Without hesitation, Emiliano rushes to Camilla and embraces her in his arms. She is exhausted from fighting the prayers and protection spells placed upon her by the priests.

Looking into her eyes with love and devotion, he promises never to let anyone harm her again. He places a passionate kiss on her lips before turning his attention back to their enemy. Realizing that there are no more living beings for Camilla to feed on for strength, Emiliano unzips his pants and offers himself to her. "Feed my love, take all the cum you need," he urges as she eagerly begins sucking him while also gaining strength from his essence.

Once Camilla has regained some of her power, Emiliano puts his cock away and turns back to face their adversary. "It's just you and me now, you bitch! I told you I would end you, and I intend to keep that promise," he bellows into the darkness.

Ammit appears within a bright glow of light, hovering above the cross on the stage. "You never learn, Emiliano. But this time, I will not only kill you, but I will also make your precious Camilla watch as I rip off her tail and use it to take her soul," she taunts as she flies towards him with tremendous speed.

Emiliano catches her by the throat as she reaches him, determined to finally defeat her once and for all. "I have learned my lesson, Ammit. And now, I am stronger than you could ever imagine," he growls as he grabs her with both hands. "I may need help to defeat you, but luckily, I have some friends here with me," he adds as black spirits begin to exit his body and attack Ammit relentlessly.

With each passing moment, they tear at her body and soul until she is weakened to a point of vulnerability. Ripping through her over and over until she is at her weakest. At Emiliano's command, they continue their assault until Ammit begins to shrink and decay before their eyes. As a final act of revenge, Emiliano leans in and gives her one last kiss before absorbing the remaining energy from her dying body.

As the glow intensifies, it transfers into Emiliano's lips and spreads throughout his entire being. He shines with a bright black light that fills the entire church. The shriveled corpse of Ammit falls lifelessly to the ground, no longer holding the soul of a goddess.

Picking up Camilla in his arms, who has now returned to her human form, Emiliano shares a tender kiss with his love before leaving the church behind them. "Siempre y para siempre mi amor! It will be just you and me for eternity," he whispers as he shoots bursts of black energy from his eyes, completely obliterating what remains of their enemy within the church walls.

As they travel down the road of the village, Emiliano ignites every building in their path. Making sure there's not a splinter of wood left standing. Emiliano continues to carry Camilla in his arms into the dark countryside. As the entire village burns behind them.

"Even after his second orgasm
drenched Camilla's core, Emiliano's demonic
erection showed no sign of relenting".

CHAPTER 18

Paloma

The car glided down an isolated country road, swallowed by the endless stretch of wilderness that seemed to go on forever. For hours, no sign of civilization had marred their journey until a hidden side road emerged, veering through dense trees like a secret passage to another world. Emiliano turned the wheel, guiding them into seclusion behind a veil of leaves, out of sight from any prying eyes.

"How do you feel, mi amor? Ready for a little snack?" Emiliano's voice dripped with anticipation as he glanced at Camilla.

She grinned mischievously. "I feel wonderful, Daddy! I thought you'd never ask."

Emiliano stepped out and spread a plush picnic blanket on the forest floor. With practiced ease, he retrieved a bottle of rich red wine, pouring a glass for each of them. After placing a lingering kiss on her lips, he murmured, "Let me fetch the main course," and sauntered to the trunk of the car.

Inside lay a beautiful young woman, naked and bound, her eyes wide with fear. Emiliano hoisted her effortlessly over his shoulder and carried her to their intimate setup.

"Our little Palomita," Camilla cooed as she traced her finger along the woman's trembling form. "You look absolutely delicious today!"

Emiliano removed her gag, letting out a scream that echoed through the trees. "Hush now, Paloma," he soothed with predatory calmness. "We wouldn't want your cries to spoil our feast." He positioned himself between her legs, his thick cock already hard and ready.

Paloma's initial cries of pain soon melded into reluctant moans of pleasure as Emiliano thrust into her mercilessly. Unable to resist any longer, Camilla slid her serpentine tail into Paloma's mouth. "Be a good girl for us," she purred. "Take it all in."

Emiliano gripped Paloma's nipples tightly as he released inside her with a primal growl. "Let's mix things up, mi amor," he suggested breathlessly as he moved behind Camilla.

He plunged deep into her pussy while she repositioned herself to penetrate Paloma's ass with her rigid tail-cock. By now, Paloma was lost in their demonic enchantment, only capable of producing wanton sounds as they ravaged her dual orifices.

Even after his second orgasm drenched Camilla's core, Emiliano's demonic erection showed no sign of relenting. Meanwhile, Camilla's climax was so intense that black cum leaked from Paloma's mouth and nose—her body convulsing in its death throes.

"Take your trophy," Camilla said with an affectionate nudge towards Paloma's lifeless breasts.

Emiliano shook his head slowly as he wiped Camilla's essence from Paloma's lips and savored it with a kiss that stole away what remained of her soul and essence. "My new trophies are far more valuable," he whispered against Camilla's lips before they packed up their dark ritual and left Paloma's empty shell behind.

They merged back onto the road hand-in-hand as Twilight embraced them. "We'll need to avoid Spain and Italy for some time," Emiliano mused aloud.

Camilla giggled softly, "How about France? Think of all the delights we could sample."

"I was thinking more about Juliette, Celine, Elise, and Genevieve," she replied playfully.

Emiliano kissed her deeply as his hand slid up her inner thigh. They shared a knowing smile as they disappeared into the descending night.

"Her beauty was a dangerous flame,
drawing you in with its allure while hiding
the sharp edge of her sadistic pleasure.
In her gaze, enchantment and
peril danced together, embodying the dark charm
of a Spanish succubus."

Adrian's Socials

Website : www.alstorytimellc.com

Email: authoradrianlopez@gmail.com

Store: www.authoradrianlopez.com

Twitter (X) handle : @berzerker1971

Youtube Podcast "Between Authors"

Weekly chat with other authors.

Channel name: alstorytimellc

Tiktok handle: @alstorytimellc

ABOUT THE AUTHOR

Adrian Lopez is a versatile author who self-publishes across multiple genres, with a primary focus on horror. His passion for the genre was ignited in his youth by the iconic classics from Universal Studios, including Dracula, Frankenstein, The Mummy, and the Wolf Man. This early fascination with these timeless monsters inspired him to craft his debut horror novella, *Lycaon Bloodlines*.

He is dedicated to presenting his stories from unique and innovative perspectives, a creative approach influenced by his admiration for Hammer Studios' reimagining of classic monsters in the 1970s. His commitment to originality and distinct storytelling is a hallmark of his work.

Horror remains a central theme in Adrian's writing, reflecting his lifelong appreciation for the genre. Each of his stories carries elements of horror, serving as a tribute to his enduring passion for the macabre and the eerie.

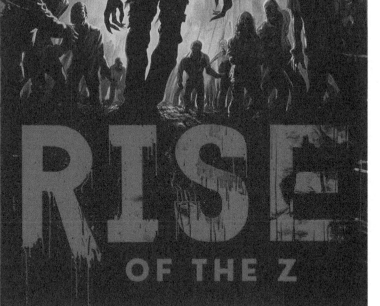

ADRIAN LOPEZ

RISE
OF THE Z

Made in United States
Orlando, FL
18 September 2024

51680503R00134